UNSPEA
EVIL

JEREMY AKERMAN

A Marc LeBlanc Mystery

Unspeakable Evil
© 2024 Jeremy Akerman

All rights reserved. No part of this book may be reproduced or transmitted in any form or by any means, electronic or mechanical, including photocopying, or by any information storage or retrieval system, without permission in writing from the publisher.

    The author expressly prohibits any entity from using this publication for purposes of training artificial intelligence (AI) technologies to generate text, including without limitation technologies that are capable of generating works in the same style or genre as this publication. The author reserves all rights to license uses of this work for generative AI training and development of machine learning language models.

Cover design: Rebekah Wetmore, from a painting by the author
Editor: Andrew Wetmore

ISBN: 978-1-998149-35-3
First edition April, 2024

2475 Perotte Road
Annapolis County, NS
B0S 1A0

moosehousepress.com
info@moosehousepress.com

We live and work in Mi'kma'ki, the ancestral and unceded territory of the Mi'kmaw people. This territory is covered by the "Treaties of Peace and Friendship" which Mi'kmaw and Wolastoqiyik (Maliseet) people first signed with the British Crown in 1725. The treaties did not deal with surrender of lands and resources but in fact recognized Mi'kmaq and Wolastoqiyik (Maliseet) title and established the rules for what was to be an ongoing relationship between nations. We are all Treaty people.

Also by Jeremy Akerman

and available from Moose House Publications

Memoir
Outsider

Politics
What Have You Done for Me Lately? - revised edition

The Marc LeBlanc Mysteries
Holy Grail, Sacred Gold
The Plot against the Premier (coming in 2024)
Best Served Cold (coming in 2024)

Fiction
Black Around the Eyes – revised edition
The Affair at Lime Hill
The Premier's Daughter
In Search of Dr. Dee
Explosion

This book is dedicated to Melanie Phillips and David Collier for their untiring efforts to expose the multitudinous libels against the Jewish people. In the face of real physical and reputational harm they have nobly gone where few others have dared to tread.

This is a work of fiction. The author has created the contemporary characters, conversations, interactions, and events; and any resemblance of any of those characters to any real person is coincidental.

Unspeakable Evil

1	9
2	12
3	19
4	23
5	31
6	35
7	47
8	52
9	60
10	63
11	69
12	75
13	82
14	90
15	95
16	99
17	109
18	117
19	127
20	132
21	137
22	145
23	150
24	157
25	166
26	170
27	179
28	189
29	200
30	205
31	210
Acknowledgements	213
About the author	215

Jeremy Akerman

1

My name is Marc LeBlanc, and my wife, Rosalie, and I had never dreamed we would become private investigators—of any kind. She had spent her time in academia, I in merchant banking. We certainly did not need any sort of activity to provide us with income because we had more than enough money from my earlier market speculations. Also, a court had recently declared my brother, Lawrence, legally dead, so I inherited my father's estate, which was worth well over a million dollars. Subsequent events might prove that some of Dad's estate was illegally gained and might have to be forfeit to the government, but even so we had something in excess of two million.

Gruelling and often frustrating though it had been, our adventure the previous year in search of the Holy Grail had given us the taste for detective work. It was true that immediately after the Grail affair we had both said "never again", but as time passed, we found we missed the excitement of fieldwork and the fascination of research. Rosalie had been fortunate to obtain a part-time assistant professorship at Acadia University, starting in the spring term, but I could tell from her restlessness that this would not be sufficient to both occupy and fulfill her.

Rosalie and I were married in August and had then gone away for several months. We spent some weeks in Paris, then in London, when we hired a car and slowly made our way through the West Country, the Cotswolds, Wales, the Lake District, the Yorkshire

Dales, up to Scotland. After some days in Edinburgh we toured up the coast to John O'Groats and down the western side. We made side trips to the Summer Isles, to Skye, Uist, Harris and Mull.

By this time the weather was getting cold and inhospitable, making us realize that we should have reversed our entire itinerary. So we went south again and picked up a little of the last mild autumn in Devon and Dorset before winding up in London, and then heading home.

It was the beginning of winter when we got back to Grand Pre, where our house is located, so we got the Bugatti Veyron Sports Vitesse out of my ultra-secure garage, and took what would be the last few drives of the year. The Bugatti has many wonderful qualities (including a world record of 408.84 kph) but, it being so low to the ground, driving in snow was definitely not one of them.

For the rest of the winter we bought a 2023 BMW 3 Series all-wheel drive which I figured we would use until the Bugatti could go back on the road sometime next May. We kept Rosalie's little Fiat because she preferred driving it to and from the university.

The other factor which rendered us susceptible to invitations to more detective work was the realization that, for all intents and purposes, I would now be idle. I did not need to work, but I needed something to make me feel in some way useful.

I had also inherited the bookstore on Main Street, but I had deeded that over to Gerald, the long-time assistant, so I knew he would not welcome my hanging around there, poking about the shelves, and getting in his way.

I did not fancy going back into banking and, in any event, there were no suitable opportunities locally. I toyed with the idea of opening a wine store, and finally set in motion the necessary steps to achieve that end, but it would take many months to find suitable premises, obtain the licenses and permits and order the inventory.

I hired a young woman, Louise LeBlanc (no relation to me) to run the place and let her get on with it. I was quarter owner of a local winery, but could not involve myself in its running for personal reasons.

For all these reasons, Rosalie and I were ready for a new adventure. We could hardly advertise, so we did not know when it would come or what it might be. When it did come, it was nothing like we imagined, and we did not dream it would lead to uncovering the most unspeakable evil either of us had ever encountered.

Jeremy Akerman

2

The circumstances which led to our new adventure occurred at a dinner party at my house. The guests were my lawyer, Walter Bryden, and his wife Joyce; my old friends Gary Marshall and his wife Jane; and Hugh Glennister. Joining them were a recent acquaintance, Ray Bland, and his fiancée, Rachel King. I had met Ray when I purchased the BMW. He owned the local franchise, and we had liked each other instantly.

Neither Rosalie nor I knew Ray very well and we had never met Rachel, so we wondered if they would fit in with our long-time friends. I rarely had more than six at my dinner parties, partly due to logistics with wine, but I expanded the numbers to nine on this occasion because I thought Ray and Rachel might be more comfortable in a larger group.

I had selected seared scallops with a caviar cream to start, then rare racks of lamb with roast potatoes and green beans, and a homemade cheesecake with a raspberry *coulis* for dessert.

I thought a 2008 Domaine des Baumard Savennieres Clos du Papillon would provide the acidity to compliment the richness of the first course, so I put three bottles of my remaining six to chill. With the lamb I wanted something rather special so opted for Diamond Creek Gravelly Meadow Cabernet Sauvignon 1998. Before dinner and with dessert, I thought we could not do better than Pol Roger Cuvee Sir Winston Churchill 1995, a Champagne which was advanced in years and had to be drunk up relatively soon, so I placed five bottles on ice.

Rosalie and I had not seen Walter, Hugh and the Marshalls since our wedding, so we were anxious to be among convivial friends again. We also were curious to know Ray better and were fascinated by his fiancée, because we had heard she was exotic in appearance and highly strung in temperament. Apparently, Ray had met her on a business visit to Montreal, when they had fallen in love and she had agreed to accompany him back to the Annapolis Valley of Nova Scotia.

For some unaccountable reason, all our guests that night had decided to attire themselves in what my mother would have called "their Sunday best," so much so that Rosalie and I felt decidedly underdressed. They arrived within minutes of each other, and soon the forecourt was full of vehicles, some of them taxis for those who appreciated my cellar.

It became immediately apparent that there was—I do not know how else to put it—a foreign body in our midst because Rachel made her presence felt in every way possible. She had a strong, yet still feminine, voice which rose above the general hubbub and was dressed exquisitely in black velvet and prominent jewellery, but most of all she looked stunning. She was about thirty, tall with a slightly olive complexion, flashing dark-brown eyes, a wide, sensual mouth and lustrous jet-black hair.

After the customary hugging and kissing of old friends re-met and the many introductions for Ray and Rachel, Rosalie took all the coats and bid the guests drift into the living room, an almost all-glass edifice with views over the fields, hill and woods beyond. When they were settled in our somewhat too sumptuous chairs and chesterfields (although they were very expensive, I had always thought them far too soft and enveloping), I set about pouring the Champagne and handing the glasses around.

I am deeply in love with Rosalie, but I have to admit I could hardly take my eyes off Rachel, and glancing around I saw that I was not alone. Only Ray seemed not to be aware of the almost hypnotic effect she had on people. She was like a queen holding court, surrounded by her devoted subjects. The extraordinary thing was that she said very little beyond a few brief pleasantries; just sat there, imperiously observing her domain.

At length we went into dinner and I poured the Savennieres while Rosalie served the scallops. There was much chattering around the table, including appreciative comments about the food, so it was not until I had emptied my plate that I realized that Rachel had not touched hers.

"Is something wrong?" I asked.

"I can't eat this," she said.

"I'm so sorry, Rachel," I said, "Are you allergic?"

"No."

"Then...?"

"Rachel is Jewish," said Ray. "Scallops are not kosher."

An embarrassed silence descended upon the table.

"Oh. You should have told us," Rosalie said. "I would have prepared something else for you."

"That's not necessary, but thank you."

"Are you okay with rack of lamb and roast potatoes?"

"Yes. I am okay with that," said Rachel with a laugh which rang around the room like quicksilver.

"And cheesecake?"

"Yes, we practically invented it. The Europeans brought their versions to North America, but it was the Jewish immigrants who came in the late 19th century who created what we call cheesecake. It is the Jewish cheesecake which is the most popular today."

"That's news to me," said Hugh.

"I imagine it is," Ruth said with a sweet smile.

"All those dietary laws. What are they called?" asked Joyce Bryden,

"Kashrut."

"Yes, Kashrut. Weren't they intended for health reasons at a time when there was no refrigeration?"

"Were they?"

"Well, weren't they?"

"I suppose eating birds of prey might be considered unhealthy. Would you eat eagles and ospreys, Mrs. Bryden?"

"No, of course not."

"How about toads and horses?"

"Well, no."

"But pigs are okay? And shellfish?"

"Yes."

"And being a vegan or a vegetarian is okay?"

"Not for me."

"But you accept it as a choice?"

"Well, yes."

"So, it is a subjective matter, not a scientific one?"

Joyce was silent.

Rachel let her stew for a minute then burst out laughing. "We will not go to war on this, Mrs. Bryden. It is just something I choose to do to honour my ancestors. I am an observant Jew to an extent. I will not eat an animal cooked in its mother's milk, but I won't wait six hours after eating meat before eating dairy products."

"Speaking of going to war," Gary Marshall butted in, "I hear you are originally from Ukraine."

"Not me, but my grandparents were," said Rachel. "They were massacred at Babi Yar."

"What's that?" Jane asked.

"A place near Kiev where Jews were shot."

"How many?" I asked.

"Estimates vary, but as many as 100,000."

"That's terrible," said Joyce. "Who did it?"

"The Nazis. They had help from Ukrainians who were Fascist sympathizers."

"Then you would have been against Canada and other western countries helping Ukraine in the war with Russia," said Gary.

"What an extraordinary thing to say," said Rachel. "I don't believe that you should invade your neighbour, no matter who it is. Why on earth would you think the murder of Jews in 1941 by people who are all dead now, would make me want to support another aggressor?"

"Sorry, Rachel." Gary said. "I wasn't thinking."

"That's the trouble. People often don't think when they are talking about Jews. They don't know what they are talking about."

"Is that fair?" I asked.

"Fair?" Rachel turned to me. "Do you think that, when you talk about Israel, Marc? Do you really know what you are talking about?"

"I think so, yes."

"I suppose you think that Israel should support a two-state solution and live in peace with the Arabs?"

"Well, yes, certainly."

"Did you know it actually happened?"

"What?"

"The two state solution."

"When?"

"In 1921.

"That's ridiculous."

"Is it? In 1920 the allies who were victorious in World War One met at San Remo in Italy and agreed to create a homeland for the Jews."

"So?"

"It was to be the whole of what is now Israel plus the whole of what is now Jordan, plus Gaza."

"Really?"

"Really."

"So what happened?"

"The British, who had been given a mandate to rule over Palestine, as the area was then called, reneged on the deal and gave two thirds of the area to Sheik Abdullah of Hejaz, now Saudi Arabia."

"Why did they do that?"

"Because Abdullah threatened to invade Syria. In order to buy him off they gave him the land that had been promised to the Jews. They called it the Emirate of Transjordan. Incidentally, to sweeten the deal, they also gave Iraq to his brother Feisal. They justified their actions by pointing to demographics showing that most people west of the Jordan River were Jews, and most people east of the river were Arabs. Voila! The two state solution."

"I never knew that." I was dumbfounded.

"I know you didn't," said Rachel. "And nor do most people. We must stop this conversation soon or your guests will be getting bored, but let me say there is something else I am sure you don't know."

"Oh. What's that?"

"That Jews have lived in what is Israel for at least 3,200 years."

"How can you possibly know that?"

"Because carved on a stone for the pharaoh of Egypt around 12,000 BCE is a reference to Israel as an independent political entity."

"Wow! But the Palestinians have been there a long time, too."

"Since 1964."

"What?"

"Until then, the Arabs refused to accept the term 'Palestinian', claiming they were part of a pan-Arab nation."

"What happened in 1964?"

"To further the Soviets' aims in the cold war, the Moscow Oriental Institute created—invented—an 'Ancient Palestinian People' for the KGB, who presented it as a gift to Arafat for the founding of the PLO."

"Good grief."

"Finally," said Rachel, "let me ask you how many times the Arabs have been offered peace, including the two-state solution."

"I don't know."

"Eight times. And every time they turned it down."

"Why?"

"Because they don't want two states. They want one state. From the river to the sea. One state from which all Jews are driven out or killed. The Hamas charter spells it out very clearly."

"Why aren't we told this?"

"Because the vast majority of the world's people, especially in the media, are anti-Semitic. Scratch them and, under the skin, you will find suspicion and hatred. It has been like that for centuries."

"Let's have some dessert!" Rosalie piped up, anxious to change the subject before we became too bogged down in serious matters.

"What an excellent idea, Rosalie," said Rachel gaily. "And more Champagne, please, Marc!"

3

When we had finished dessert we all moved back into the living room and relaxed. Joyce, Rachel and Rosalie just had coffee, while Hugh, Jane and I had glasses of Courvoisier XO Royal Cognac. Ray and Walter settled for Glenturret, Triple Wood 2022 Single Malt.

"I give you Marc and Rosalie," said Walter, raising his glass.

"Detectives extraordinary and finders of the Holy Grail."

"What is this?" Rachel asked.

"Marc and Rosalie had a great adventure last year. They actually tracked down the Holy Grail itself."

"You're joking!"

"No, it's a fact. It took them some time, but they did it despite some awful setbacks."

"Yeah, especially that day in the barrens of Cape Breton," I said. "I've still got scars where the deer flies ate me alive."

"This is utterly fascinating. It's like something from a fantasy novel," said Rachel. "I want to hear the whole story sometime. Will you tell it to me, Rosalie and Marc?"

"Sometime, yes."

"Thank you. I would enjoy that."

"Incidentally, Marc," Gary said, as he stretched out in his arm chair, "Commiserations on your dad."

"Did your father die recently?" Rachel asked. "I'm so sorry."

"Yes, last year. But I think Gary means something different."

"Oh, I'm sorry, Marc. It was tactless of me to bring it up."

"I don't understand," said Rachel.

"It's not a problem," I said. "It's just that sometime after my father died we found out he was a criminal."

"How extraordinary. If I may say so, you don't seem all that bothered about it."

"Actually it does bother me, Rachel, but I know there's nothing I can do about it now. So I have to accept it and move on."

"I am sure that is the wisest course." She turned and gave Ray a knowing look. "Ray, darling. Should we tell them?"

Ray looked embarrassed and shifted uneasily in his seat.

"What is this about?" Rosalie asked.

"Ray has mysterious relatives too," said Rachel. "Tell them, honey."

"It's my grandfather," Ray said hesitantly.

"Your grandfather?"

"Yes, my father's father. He was a huge mystery. At least, that is the impression I got. I didn't know him well because he died when I was a kid. My father steadfastly refused to talk about him, but my mother was full of remarks about him, none of them favourable."

"Like what?"

"Snide comments, mostly. Implications that he was up to no good. Raising questions about his origins. That sort of thing."

"That's fascinating," said Rosalie.

"My mother implied that nobody knew where he was born, where he came from or how he got to be in Paradise."

"Paradise?"

"Yes, it's a small community between Lawrencetown and Bridgetown in Annapolis County."

"What did he do for a living?"

"He was a doctor. A family physician. He also did some painting."

"Wait a minute," said Hugh. "What was his name?"

"John Bland," said Ray.

"Right! He was a painter of some note. I have one of his works at home. It's very good."

"Yes, I heard that he was a respected landscape painter. His paintings are all over the place. Many are in galleries and museums."

"Were the landscapes of places here in the Valley?"

"Not all of them. Apparently he toured all over the province, painting country scenes, whenever he could get away from his practice."

"I see," I said. "Does it trouble you that you don't know anything about this man?"

"Yes, it does," Ray said, with sudden vehemence. "After all he was my own flesh and blood. I should know more than I do."

"Maybe Rosalie and Marc could find out for you," said Rachel. "They have the experience and the expertise."

"No, no. I couldn't impose on them."

The room was silent. Rosalie and I looked at each other. She gave me a strange look which was her way of saying: "if it's alright with you, it's alright with me."

"What do you say, Marc, Rosalie?" Rachel was insistent.

"Before we agree, you must understand that there is no guarantee that what we would find would be good. In fact the reverse is probably the case."

"Sometimes it's better to let sleeping dogs lie," said Rosalie.

"I understand," said Ray, "but I think I need to know."

"Alright then, we'll do it."

"Would it be expensive?"

"Ray! We are amateurs. There would be no charge, except maybe for any extraordinary expenses we might incur."

"Wonderful!" Rachel exclaimed. "Come to our place for dinner tomorrow and you can get all the details."

"Thank you. We will."

Jeremy Akerman

"Well," said Walter, rising. "Another toast is in order. To the next adventure of the Detectives of Grand Pre."

4

Rachel and Ray lived in a large house in Port Williams which I guessed was about a hundred and fifty years old. It had a big wrap-around porch and a widow's walk, and was painted sparkling white with dark green trim. In front and behind were rolling, manicured lawns edged with roses, peonies, phlox and gladioli. At the far end of the property was a large plot of herbs and vegetables.

Rosalie and I took a taxi there, as I suspected it would be a long night with a fair amount of wine consumption. Ray was a relatively recent recruit to wine appreciation, but had taken to it with alacrity and with no expense spared.

Shortly after arriving, we learned that they had only lately moved into the house following Ray's mother's having passed away at the age of 73 the previous fall. His father, Edgar, died in 2012, aged 64. His grandfather had bought the house and moved from Paradise, some 70 kilometres away, when Edgar was born.

The house was splendid inside, with much of the original wood panelling and staircases still intact and gleaming with the comforting patina of age. Ray's mother had continued her mother-in-law's practice of festooning the large windows with voluminous lace curtains. The future of these was now a subject of debate within the household, Rachel desiring them gone, Ray wanting to keep them for old time's sake.

Rachel had prepared a simple but delicious dinner. First, we had soup made from spring onions and herbs from the garden; followed by cold poached salmon with small, new, hot buttered potatoes; and a selection of chocolate babka, mandel bread and halva for dessert.

Ray, still learning his wines but wanting to impress, served Taittinger Brut Champagne and a Grgich Hills Estate Chardonnay from the 2016 vintage. He said he didn't know what to serve with the lusciously sweet desserts, so had more Champagne if we wanted.

We had a very pleasant meal, keeping the conversation light for the most part, and reserving the business until after the meal. I did, however, steer the discourse to serious matters towards the end when I tackled Rachel about what she had said the previous night about widespread, ingrained anti-Semitism.

"It is not anti-Semitic to be opposed to policies of the Israeli government," I said.

"Well," she said taking a deep breath, "in my experience most people who assert that are anti-Semites, especially if subsequent investigation reveals that they oppose every policy of the Israeli government, and most definitely if they oppose the existence of a Jewish state."

"I suppose they can if they wish."

"Marc, there are 195 countries in the world. Anyone who begrudges the Jews just one tiny country half the size of Nova Scotia must be doing so because they hate Jews."

"But if someone is against the principle of states predicated upon religion, criticizing Israel would not necessarily be anti-Semitic?"

"*If,*" she said with great emphasis, "But would they also be opposed, and give expression to that opposition, in the case of fifty-six Islamic countries and another twenty-four based on various other religions? But how often do you hear people condemning Israel and how often do you hear them condemning the other eighty countries?"

"Well, yes," I conceded, "you have a point there. But what about charges that Israel is apartheid?"

"In what way?"

"Er...I guess by discriminating against the Palestinians."

"How are they discriminated against?"

"Well...I'm not quite sure, but we see it in the media all the time."

"Which was the point I made last night. But let us examine the charge. In Israel there are about two million Arabs—we established last night there is no such thing as a Palestinian—living in Israel, where they have full rights in all matters, including voting rights. There are another three million living in what you call the 'West Bank', where they are virtually independent from Israel and are governed by the Palestinian Authority, but where they do not have the vote."

"What? What do you mean? Wasn't Mahmoud Abbas democratically elected president?"

"Yes, he was, in 2005, but then he abolished elections. So he is now serving in the eighteenth year of a four year term."

"I had no idea."

"No, you didn't. But you are right if you say there is apartheid in Israel."

"Ah," I said, leading with my chin.

"And do you know who practices it?"

"I'm sure you're going to tell me."

"Yes I am, Marc. It is practised by the Palestinian Authority, which does not permit Jews to live anywhere within their jurisdiction or to enter most of what historically were two of the Jews' most ancient provinces."

"Is that the West Bank?"

"The 'West Bank' my dear Marc, are Judea and Samaria. Sound familiar from your Bible studies at Sunday School? They have only been called the West Bank since 1948, when the Jordanian army illegally occupied them. Jordan called the area the West Bank because it was territory they seized on the west side of the River Jordan. At which time, incidentally, they expelled the Jews."

"But they are now back in Israel?"

"Yes because in 1967, the Israeli army took them back from Jordan. But the Arabs were allowed to remain."

"Come on you guys," Rosalie interrupted, "enough of this argy-bargy. We're getting way too serious here."

"Okay, Rosalie. I apologize," said Rachel, "but I have an idea that what we have to discuss now will be just as serious in its own way."

"We may as well get to it," said Ray. "What do you want to know?"

"Okay. Let's start at the beginning," I said. "Rosalie, will you take notes, please?"

"Sure. Ready when you are."

"What was your grandfather's full name?"

"John Bland. As far as I know he didn't have a middle name."

"That's unusual. When was he born?"

"We don't know, but on his death certificate it said he was 80. I guess Dad put that down, but I'm sure he was only guessing."

"Did he not have birthdays throughout his life? Didn't they record his age?"

"Don't know. I was only seven when he died. I can't remember anything like that."

"Do we know where he was born?"

"No. Dad thought it was in Holland but, again, that was a guess because apparently he got his medical degree there."

"Where?"

"I saw his certificate, but it was a long time ago. I'm not a hundred percent sure, but I think it was Leiden."

"When did he first start his medical practice in....Paradise, was it?"

"Yes, Paradise. I'm not sure, but it must have been in the forties because Dad was born in 1948."

"Did he practice medicine from the beginning of his time in Paradise, or was he there for some time prior?"

"I have no idea. Sorry."

"Okay. Whom did he marry? That is, who was your paternal grandmother?"

"Her name was Ida Murchison."

"Do you know how old she was when they married?"

"I think she was twenty. It must have been around 1945."

"It would be easy to check that in the province's Vital Statistics," said Rosalie.

"Right. What do we know about Ida?"

"Let me see. I seem to remember she came from a large family in West Paradise."

"Do you recall how many siblings she had?"

"Five I think. I remember Mom said two of them died young. I seem to recall they were both girls."

"Accidents, or something like influenza?"

"No, she said they had a mysterious disease."

"How mysterious?"

"I can't remember. Mom just said they died before their time."

"Were all the siblings younger than Ida?"

"I'm not sure. I have an idea that one, a brother, was older."

"Ray, might I have another glass of Champagne? Cross examining is thirsty work!"

"Sure. Rachel, would you get it, darling, please?"

"Of course," said Rachel, getting up and going to the fridge.

"Alright. Now then. How many children did John and Ida have?"

"That I *am* sure of. They were four, and one who died very young. Or maybe it was a miscarriage."

"Where was your dad in the order?"

"He was number three."

"Are any still alive?"

"No. The second to be born was the last to die. His name was Oscar. He died in 2019. He was 70 when he died. Pneumonia, I think. We didn't have much to do with him. I think I only ever saw him two or three times."

"What happened to the others?"

"Let me think. Yes, the first born was Hilda. She died when she was 12 or 13."

"What about the youngest?"

"That would have been Heather. She died long before I was born. Sometime in the 1960s, I think."

"Do you know the cause of her death?"

"I think it was the same problem as Hilda. Or so my mother intimated."

"They would both have been 13 when they died," Rosalie interposed.

"Extraordinary. You have no idea what the medical condition was?"

"No, sorry. But I recall my mother hinting that it was the same thing that killed Ida's sisters."

"Is that how she put it?"

"How do you mean?"

"Were those her exact words: 'the same thing that killed Ida's sisters'?"

"I think so. I can't be sure after all this time. It was something like that."

"Okay." I took a sip of my champagne. "Now tell me about your grandfather's paintings."

"Apparently, he was very good. That one over there is his." Ray pointed to the far wall, where a picture of a rural scene of a bridge and a wheat field hung.

I got up and walked across the room. It was entitled *Summer Near Moschelle*. I am no expert, but I could immediately tell that the painting was technically very sound, the attention to detail being uncanny. However, to me, it lacked something—life, for want of a better word—and seemed somewhat mechanical. But I could see why his work was admired and why he might be able to get good prices for his paintings.

"Where's Moschelle?" I asked Ray.

"It's down near Annapolis Royal."

"Were they all landscapes?"

"Yes. I seem to remember my father mentioning that in summer they would pack up and go camping in various parts of the province. That's when he did his painting. What do they call it?"

"*En plein air*," volunteered Rachel.

"Yes, that's it. It means he did all of them from life. He may have touched them up later, but I don't know for sure."

"Do we know how many paintings he did?"

"Oh no, but I would guess over fifty. There's one in the Art Gallery of Nova Scotia in Halifax."

"Did he sell them?"

"Sometimes. But there were some he wouldn't sell. I guess he liked them too much to part with them."

"Are there any more here in this house?"

"Yes, one is in a closet with a bunch of other stuff. Mom hated it. I never knew why. That's why she shut it away. She only allowed that one to stay on the wall because it was a favourite of Dad's."

"May we see the other one, please, Ray?"

"Sure. I'll go get it."

He went to the back of the house, rummaged around in an old closet, and came back with a rather ominous looking painting of the Tantramar marshes on an overcast day with dark clouds on the

Jeremy Akerman

horizon. This one was called *Gathering Storm, near Fort Lawrence*. I actually liked it better than the other one, but even this one had a mechanical feel about it. I could not fully explain it, even to myself, but, despite the amount of technical skill displayed, I formed the impression that the painting was somehow incomplete.

"Do you happen to know what kind of prices he got for the ones he sold?"

"Oh. I think I heard Dad say that his father had once been offered $300, but when that was I have no idea."

"Thank you, Ray. Rosalie, do you have any questions?"

"Not tonight," she said, "but I'm sure we will have more as time goes on."

"Yes. We must go. Rachel, could you please call us a taxi? We had a wonderful dinner."

"I'm sure we'll be seeing more of you quite often," she replied.

"Yes, we'll give you regular updates."

5

The next morning, just as Rosalie and I were about to sit down to a leisurely breakfast of fresh croissants, mushroom omelettes and Blue Mountain coffee, the phone rang.

"Marc, it's Ray. Last night there's something I should have mentioned to you."

"Hi, Ray. What was that?"

"I forgot all about it. There's a bunch of things up in the attic which look as if they have been there for years. It may have been Dads' stuff, but then again at least some of it may be my grandfather's belongings."

"That sounds promising."

"I've only taken a quick peek, but the stuff is piled up at one end of the attic about three feet deep. And it's covered with dust."

"Well, we figured on getting our hands dirty…one way or another."

"So you'll come over?"

"Certainly."

"When? How about tonight?"

"Can't tonight. How about we come over tomorrow evening?"

"Or you could come in the daytime. I can get a key for you."

"No, you'd need to be there, so we will be able to distinguish the later material which belonged to your father and mother from what was your grandfather's."

"Right. Okay tomorrow evening."

"See you then."

Rosalie was already tucking into her omelette when I got back to the table. Mine was starting to cool, but it was very tasty so I made short work of it.

While I was slathering unpasteurized Nova Scotia Nectar honey onto my croissant, Rosalie said, "Coincidence or what?"

"What are you talking about?"

She held up the jar and showed me the label. The honey was made at a farm in Paradise. "Maybe it's a sign that our efforts will be successful."

"Let us hope so," I said. "Does your pal Trudy still work for Doctors Nova Scotia?"

"Yes."

"Why don't you call her and see if she can find any records on John Bland?"

"I will. As soon as I've finished my coffee."

~

When she contacted Trudy, who was an administrator at Doctors Nova Scotia, the successor to the Nova Scotia Medical Society, she told Rosalie that her computerized records did not go back far enough, but that she would get the information to her within the hour.

While we were waiting for the call, I told Rosalie what Ray had said, and we speculated on what we might find.

"Why is John Bland a mystery?" I asked.

"When you get right down to it, it is only because Ray's mother made some slighting remarks about him, and because Ray's father didn't like to talk about him."

"Exactly. For all we know, the man may have been as pure as the driven snow."

"And even if he wasn't, why on earth would he keep any records which might have incriminated him?"

"Indeed. What do you think we'll find in that attic?"

"Junk, I expect. Mostly. Maybe old documents which no longer have any relevance. Boxes of ancient magazines. Maybe unwanted gifts from Christmases past. Bits and pieces nobody wanted to throw out. I don't hold out much hope."

The phone rang. It was Trudy. She said that records from wartime were poor, and few and far between, but she had located a John Bland, aged 28, of Paradise, Annapolis County, who was licensed in 1943. She said his credential from Leiden University in the Netherlands was in the record, but that it was not wholly convincing.

"What did she mean by that?" I asked.

"She said some of the ink appeared to have run on the certificate. But she didn't have the original so couldn't be sure."

"Did you ask if there was a shortage of doctors during WWII?"

"Great minds think alike!" she said, "Yes, I did. She said a large number of younger doctors would have joined up and gone overseas to serve in the fighting forces, which would have left a shortage of physicians for the civilian population."

"And...?"

"She allowed as to how under those conditions, the authorities might not have scrutinized applications as strictly as they might have done in peacetime. And she said she was only guessing, but that with everything in chaos due to the war, a lowly official might possibly have turned a blind eye to irregularities either because of the burden of work, or for a small consideration."

"A bribe."

"Precisely."

"So, at least we know Ray was right about it having been Leiden."

Jeremy Akerman

"But that's all we know."

"It is more than possible that there is nothing else to know," I said rather morosely.

6

The next day we met Ray at the house at around five o'clock. He said that Rachel, who was a hospital administrator, would be at work until later, but she had said we should again stay and have dinner with them.

Ray let us in and, stopping first to get a wet cloth which he put into a plastic bag, led us up the main staircase, which creaked the way all old staircases should, and then up two much narrower, uncarpeted sets of stairs until we came to two doors, each about five feet high.

"That leads to the widow's walk," said Ray, indicating the door on the right. "Do you want to take a look?"

"Sure. That would be nice," said Rosalie.

We stooped and crowded through into a space which spanned the width of the house, but which was no more than four feet wide. I was amazed at how high up we were and how much we could see. There were small widows all the way along, giving a panoramic view of the Cornwallis estuary, the bay and beyond in one direction Starr's Point and in the other North Grand Pre.

In the centre of this gallery was a small gable which protruded high above the front door, from which, presumably, the eponymous widow could squeeze in to get a clearer sight to the sea.

"This is the first time I've been in here in about twenty-five years," Ray said. "It sure could do with a good clean. This dust must be a quarter of an inch thick."

"When did you and your family move in here?" I asked.

"The first time would have been when my grandfather died in 1995. I was seven. I moved out when I was 18 to go to college and didn't come back until last year."

"So John Bland would have lived here for almost fifty years?" said Rosalie.

"Yes, that sounds about right."

I walked up the gallery to the seaward end and stopped suddenly when I saw a dirt-encrusted object attached to the window ledge. I did not have to get my hands filthy in order to see that it was a telescope and, by the look of it, a very powerful one.

"Did your grandfather enjoy looking at the ocean?"

"Not after 1978 he didn't. He couldn't have."

"What happened in 1978?"

"He had a car accident and was confined in a wheelchair until his death in '95."

"Yes," said Rosalie with conviction, "it would be difficult to get a wheel chair up those stairs!"

"When did his wife die? What was her name?"

"Ida."

"Yes Ida. When did she go?"

"Oh, a long time before he did. Over twenty years, I think. She was in her forties when she died."

"Do we know why?"

"Why what?"

"Sorry, I meant what the cause of death."

"Oh. Um…it was well before I was born. I forget. I can see if I can find her death certificate."

"Thanks."

"Shall we go into the attic now?"

"Sure."

We backed out of the widow's walk, awkwardly paused on the

tiny landing while Ray struggled with the key, then stumbled into the attic.

"Excuse me, Ray, but why was it locked?"

"Er...don't know. It just was. I won't continue the practice."

He pulled a string to switch on a single overhead bulb, then pointed to the other end of the loft. There was a pile of boxes, papers, pictures and odd bits of furniture.

Ray took a broom which was standing in the corner and approached the assemblage. "Better stand back," he said. "This could be dirty."

He was right. Clouds of dust billowed into the air, settling among the beams of the roof. It was so bad that Rosalie ducked out and waited on the landing.

At length, Ray took out his wet cloth and wiped the tops of the boxes. Within seconds the cloth was filthy and he distastefully dropped it back in the bag.

"Uggh! Would you rather come back after I've given it a proper cleaning?"

"No. We're here now. We may as well get on with it."

"Alright. How do you want to proceed, Marc?"

"One by one, take each box or bundle, indicating if you think it's relevant. The ones which are not relevant should go to the other side, on the left> Put the ones which might be useful by the door."

"Okay." He said, dragging a box from the stack. "This is full of knitting patterns. Those would have been my mother's."

"Right, Rosalie, could you put it over there, please?"

"And this seems to contain magazines."

"What is the date of the oldest one?"

"Let me see...er...seems to be 2015."

"Okay, Rosalie, another for your pile."

"This one has clothes in it...and...ugh...moth balls!"

"Whose were they?"

"Judging from the styles they would also be Mum's."

"My pile is growing," said Rosalie. "So, nothing useful yet."

"Here are some of Granddad's paintings, still in their frames. These are heavy. Marc, can you help me with them?"

"Sure. I think we had better take these downstairs, clean them up and then take a close look at them. If I pass each one to you Rosalie, could you put them out on the landing?"

"Okay, but we'll soon run out of space. I think I'd better taken them down, one at a time."

There turned out to be five paintings, which we carefully stacked on the landing. Rosalie then carried them downstairs.

"What's next, Ray?"

"More clothes. Also Mum's."

"Ok let me have that. I'll put in the useless pile."

"Newspapers. Can't think why anyone would want to keep them."

"Dates?"

"Er...the earliest appears to be...in the 1990s...yes 1998. That was when Granddad died."

"They may contain his obituary, so we'd better hang on to those. Next."

"Three...no four...rolled up carpets. I'll need your help again with these, Marc."

"Alright. Jesus, these are filthy! What are they doing here?"

"Mum was a packrat. She couldn't bear to throw anything out. She used to say: 'You never know when we might need it'."

We dragged the carpets to the useless pile and realized that now that pile was bigger than the remaining items.

"Here's a box of papers," said Ray.

"What are they?"

"They seem to be copies of returns to the provincial Medical Services Insurance. The last of them is in 1988. I think that's when he stopped practising medicine. He would have been in his seventies then, I think."

"We'd better take those."

"Wow!" Ray's exclamation was so loud that I whirled around, and Rosalie came scurrying into the attic.

Ray had just pulled a black cloth away from some items which had been laid against the back wall. There were a large metal strongbox and a huge iron safe. The box, measuring about three feet deep by two and a half feet square, was black. The safe, also black, was a full five feet tall, four feet wide and three feet deep. There was a light covering of dust on each, but beneath, one could see that the metal was shiny. We gaped in astonishment.

"This is interesting!" Rosalie said.

"You don't happen to have the keys, Ray?"

"'Fraid not. I had no idea these were here. And I doubt that mother did, either."

"How about your father?"

"He may have, but he might not have had the keys. I'll hunt around—look in drawers and vases—but my guess is they are long gone now."

"We'll need professional help getting in to them," I said.

"Very professional help," Rosalie said. "These things are enormous."

She went to the box and kicked it, and it rocked ever so slightly. She pushed hard on the safe, but it did not move.

"I'll have a word with my neighbour, Tim, to help me with the box when he gets back from vacation." Ray said. "He has a cut-off saw. I'll ask him if he has a metal-cutting blade. But the safe is a whole different matter."

"I'll talk to the locksmith in New Minas and see what he says. Ray, could you clean off the panel where it gives the make and type."

Reluctantly, Ray dipped back into his plastic bag, withdrew the cloth and rubbed it over the front of the safe.

"Marc, could you light up your phone so I can see it better?"

"Sure."

"Okay. It says, 'The Major 100 SureLock. Underneath in smaller letters is 12 gauge steel. 12 x 1.5" locking bolts'. Then what looks like 'TRTL-30'."

"Did you get that, Rosalie?"

"All duly noted."

"Let's go down. I'm almost choking with all this dust."

We traipsed downstairs, awkwardly lugging the newspapers and MSI returns. We got back just as Rachel was coming through the front door.

"What have you been doing?" She asked. "You're filthy. You look like you've been playing in the farmyard!"

"Sorry, darling," said Ray. "Can we have some towels, please? Rosalie and Marc can clean up in the back bathroom. I'll get a wash and change. What's for dinner?"

"I'm back from work only two minutes and you ask me that?" She laughed. "It'll be all cold. I picked up some cooked meats and fresh bread at the delicatessen and we have some cheese in the fridge. I'll duck out into the garden and get some scallions and lettuce."

"Sounds wonderful, Rachel," Rosalie chimed. "I'm starving!"

"Ray, honey, what wine should I put in to chill?"

"Bring up a bottle of that Meursault and one of the Fleurie. But don't chill the Fleurie."

"Aright. Now, you lot, go and make yourselves presentable."

Twenty minutes later we were seated around the dining room table, which was covered with a dazzling white cloth. Rachel had set out a basket of sliced, crusty bread, a pot of butter, plates of cold roast beef and turkey, four different cheeses, and a big bowl of green salad.

We told Rachel about our discovery and of our doubts about accessing at least the safe.

"How weird," she said. "They have been sitting up in that attic for at least 30 years. However did your grandfather get them up there in the first place?"

"That's a good point," I said. "I suppose that, if he'd had help, two men could get the strong box up there, but I can't imagine how they handled the safe."

"If they attached a pulley to the gable in the widow's walk, could he have got it in that way?" Rosalie asked.

"I don't think so," said Ray. "The window's too small. And how could they have manoeuvred it from the widow's walk across the landing into the attic?"

"I don't think how he got it there is crucial to our purposes, but what is inside," I interposed. "My guess is that, if you could get a builder or an architect to examine the building, you'd likely find that your grandfather had a shaft installed to haul it up. Then once it was in position, he had the affected rooms restored to their previous states."

"God, there must have been gold bars in that safe if he went to all that trouble."

"Ray," I said, something having just occurred to me. "Do you have a photograph of your grandfather?"

"Yes, there's one in the back room closet, I think. I'll fetch it."

We heard him rummaging around and then he came back looking puzzled.

"It's not there. I distinctly remember seeing it there about a few years ago. My mother sent me to get something and I saw it at that time."

"Did you tell her that you had found it?"

"Yes, I did."

"There's your answer. I'll bet dollars to doughnuts that after you'd gone she destroyed it."

"I hadn't thought of that."

"She really had a hate on for him, didn't she?" Rachel asked.

"She sure didn't like him, but I don't know if it was hate."

For several minutes we busied ourselves with the delicious food and wine. While I sometimes went to great lengths to put on elaborate meals, I often thought that good ingredients simply presented were the most memorable. This repast had been put together in about half an hour and was quite exquisite. The wines, too, were excellent choices for the occasion.

"Speaking of hatred," I said, "I wanted to follow up on our discussion of the other night. Is that okay?"

"Certainly."

"Two matters have me puzzled."

"Fire away."

"You said something about giving land to the Palestinians—"

"The Arabs."

"Yes, the Arabs. You said that it wasn't about land at all."

"It isn't. It's about religion, and getting complete control of the region, then kicking the Jews out or killing them."

"I know you said this was in the Hamas Charter, but do you have solid examples of this?"

"Sure. Gaza. In 2005, Ariel Sharon gave Gaza to the Arabs, even expelling all 8,500 Jews who lived there. He called it 'Land for Peace.'"

"So?"

"Did he get peace? No. The Arabs chose Hamas to rule them and have fired more than 20,000 Iranian-supplied rockets from Gaza into Israel since then. He gave the land, but didn't get the peace."

"That's not quite the way we've heard it in our media."

"Of course not. The media as a collectivity is anti-Semitic. They are Jew-haters at heart."

"Isn't that putting it a little strongly?"

"Is it? What about the media's handling of the events of October 7th last year? You must remember Hamas' monstrous massacre of more than 1,100 Israelis at the Kibbutz Be'eri?"

"I heard it was only 360."

"360 who actually participated in the music festival, but another 800 were slaughtered by Hamas in the surrounding area."

"Oh."

"The United Nations investigation found that dozens of sexual crimes were committed, including violent acts of rape, with weapons in some cases aimed at wounded women. Mass rapes occurred, often intentionally committed in front of husbands, partners and family members to maximize the pain and helplessness felt and increase the terror. Hamas carried out a hunting expedition to catch young men and women who attempted to escape the carnage, dragging them by the hair. The sexual violence targeted men, women and girls and included binding their bodies, mutilating genitals and the bodies of both males and females with knives and in some cases inserting weapons inside the genitals. In most cases, the victims were executed, either during the rape or after."

"I didn't know the details," I said rather sheepishly.

"And people were beheaded. I saw last night with my own eyes a video—taken by Hamas—of a man's head being cut off with a spade. There was even a report that Hamas roasted a baby in an oven. Dozens of bodies were burned beyond recognition."

"Why would Hamas take footage of their own crimes?"

"Because they are proud of their crimes. They boasted of them in phone messages to relatives. Even the Nazis tried to cover up their crimes. Hamas gloried in theirs."

"Awful. I guess all this will not easily be forgotten."

"But most people did forget it, and especially the media. Or at least they buried it. Within 24 hours the media completely turned the story around and made it all about the so-called 'innocent Palestinian civilians', many of whom actually participated in the massacre and most of whom joyfully celebrated it in the streets. In less than a day the massacre became Israel's fault even though they were the victims. Can you think of another example where the side that started a war was portrayed as the victim?"

"I guess not."

"And can you think of another example when the media concerned itself almost exclusively with the 'civilians' of the belligerent?"

"Well, um...."

"Germany or Japan in WWII?"

"No, of course not."

"How about Iraq, following their invasion of Kuwait?"

"No, I guess not."

"Afghanistan after 911?"

"No."

"North Korea in 1950 after they invaded South Korea?"

"No."

"And did ever witness the media rushing to print lies which would portray one side in such a negative light?"

"What do you mean?"

"Do you not recall when a Hamas rocket misfired and hit a hospital parking lot, but most of the media reported that Israeli air force had attacked the hospital itself, killing children?"

"Ah, yes."

"Did any of them subsequently apologize for printing lies in that or in any other false story?"

"I guess not."

"And did you ever witness such positive media coverage of

Unspeakable Evil

worldwide, blood-thirsty, pro-Hamas demonstrations justifying the massacre?"

"No, I guess not, but what about the Nakba?"

"I understand that you'd rather not talk about the Massacre. Well, what about Nakba?"

"Why did Israel do it?"

"Let me see. You have heard or read that Israel expelled 700,000 Arabs from the land and that is why millions of them are now living in refugee camps."

"Well...er...yes."

"When Israel declared its independence from Britain in May of 1948, she was attacked by the armies of seven—that's seven—countries. They were so sure they would be successful that they told the Arabs to leave Israel so as not to get in the way of the invading armies. They told the Arabs that after they had won the war, they could return, get their own properties back and have the Jews' lands as well. So most of them left."

"What happened?"

"They lost. The Jews beat them. All the invaders got was Judea and Samaria—what you call 'the West Bank'. When the Arabs asked the seven belligerent countries if they could stay in the countries to which they had fled, they were told they had to go into camps—where they have been ever since."

"But—"

"Wait! I'm not finished! There were 700,000 in 1948 but there are 1.5 million in the camps today. The only 'genocide' in history in which the population doubled!"

"We're not told this," I said feebly.

"No Marc, you are not. But there's more. From the Arab countries there were over 800,000 Jews who were expelled and who fled to Israel, where their descendants reside today. Do you know how many Jews there are in Egypt now?"

45

"I don't know."

"One hundred. How about Lebanon?"

"Don't know."

"One hundred. Yemen and Aden?'

I shook my head.

"Fifty. Iraq? Seven. Algeria? Fifty. Syria? 100. Bahrain? 36. Bangladesh? 75. Afghanistan? Zero. Libya? Zero. Sudan? Zero!"

"I'm sorry."

"Better you should be informed than sorry," said Rachel. "But let's have more wine. If we are to become safe crackers, we must be well fortified!"

7

The following day I had an appointment with one Jerry Swift, who was Curator of Nova Scotian Art at the provincial Art Gallery in Halifax. I was not sure what I hoped to gain from meeting him, but at least I figured he might have a complete list of Bland's paintings and where they were now. I had recently had the Bugatti completely serviced, as summer was already upon us, so I thought a clear run to Halifax might do it good.

Swift was a man in his forties, with long hair and a long beard, and was dressed in jeans and a plaid shirt. He spoke with a semi-whine as though he were seeing me under protest, and started every sentence as if he were defending a sacred proposition against Philistine hordes.

"Bland is certainly not one of the greats, you understand," he said, "but for this province he's not bad if you like that sort of thing."

"You're not from Nova Scotia?"

"Ontario." He sniffed. "His oeuvre would hardly be noted there, of course, but as local landscape artists go, I guess he was popular in his day."

"You don't like his work?"

"Not at all. I find it...dead...if you know what I mean."

"I think I do," I said, regretting that I was agreeing with this rather unpleasant character. "Mechanical is the word which came to my mind."

"That would serve. Yes, mechanical. If you were inclined to be romantic, you might say his work lacks soul."

"How many paintings did he produce?"

"Of course, we can't possibly account for those he might have destroyed, or painted over, or indeed any he simply didn't put on the market."

"No, of course not."

"I have tracked 35 for certain, and we think there might be another dozen out there which, for whatever reasons, were not recorded."

"Do you have a record of *Summer near Moschelle* or *Gathering Storm near Fort Lawrence*?"

"What? I don't think I know those." He made it sound like an accusation. "Let me look…mmm…no, I don't have those on my list. Have you seen them?"

"Yes."

"Are you sure they are his?"

"I am no expert, Mr. Swift, but—"

"Doctor Swift," he corrected me with some force.

"I'm sorry. But they have been in the house he owned for some fifty years and, as far as anyone knows, have never been anywhere else."

"I suppose that's some kind of provenance." He sniffed again. "Are there any more?"

"Yes, five. I haven't had a chance to properly study them yet. They are filthy."

"Well, for God's sake, don't clean them unless you know what you're doing! It's a special skill, you know."

"I was aware of that," I said, perhaps a little too icily. "I was going to ask you if I could bring them here to be cleaned."

"Ah…that's a bit tricky. We don't actually provide that service to the general public."

"Well, we have to get them cleaned professionally and I wouldn't know where else to go. If I could persuade my friend—on whose behalf I'm acting in this—to donate one of them to the gallery, would that be adequate compensation?"

"That would be a different matter. Can you call him?"

"Yes. If you'll excuse me for a few minutes I'll do it now."

I got Ray at the dealership and put the idea to him. He immediately agreed, and said he would get one of his employees to deliver them to Dr. Swift the following day.

"But which one should we give him? Should we let him choose?" he asked.

"I suggest you have them cleaned first, then give the gallery the one you like least."

"Fair enough. But what if I don't like any of them? You know I'm not comfortable with anything to do with him."

"In that case, it can be his choice. You might decide to donate them all, or sell them to the gallery. I could suggest that if you like."

"How about you tell him to go ahead with the cleaning and, unless I fancy a particular painting, he can have them all? One as a donation and the others for a nominal consideration."

"I'll try it."

"Okay. Are you going to be around tomorrow?"

"No, I thought Rosalie and I would wander down to Paradise."

"Right. Let me know how you get on."

Swift seemed totally disconcerted by Ray's offer and needed me to explain it carefully, which I did.

"Ah, I see. So the gallery gets one as a donation, and we compensate him for the others?"

"Pretty much."

"I'll have to go to the Acquisitions Committee for approval. If they go for it, I doubt they will agree to pay the market value. Their budget is ludicrously small. I could say, criminally small!"

"I have a feeling Mr. Bland will go along with any reasonable offer. He might even throw in the first two I mentioned."

"Bland? But that's the painter's name."

"Yes, he is the painter's grandson."

"Oh. I see. Alright. Leave it with me and I'll get back to you. Is there anything else?"

"Yes, you said you thought Bland's work was dead—I think that was the word you used. I wonder if you could enlarge upon that?"

"Certainly. Come with me."

I followed him down a corridor, then through a small door and out into the gallery. Over in a corner were hanging four paintings which, even to my inexpert eye, were unmistakably the work of John Bland.

"Come here," Swift commanded. "Look at this. He's highly proficient technically, and I often wonder whether, if he managed to persevere longer, his technical ability might have carried him through. Understand?"

"Not entirely."

"Look here. A perfectly passable farmer's yard with the hay barn beyond, but look at the ground. Not the same degree of detail. It's almost as if he got tired and just quit. The same with this one. A seascape. Look at those waves! Quite brilliant in its own way. Yet examine the rocks. They look like cardboard. Again it's like he lost interest before finishing."

"Or was in a rush?"

"Or in a hurry. Yes, it could be. Don't get me wrong, even if this—what shall we call it?—unfinished quality didn't exist, I still wouldn't care for his stuff. There's no empathy for nature. No enthusiasm."

"Yes, I agree. That's what I would say, too."

"Well there you are. Anything else?"

"Yes, I would like a copy of your list of his known works, and where they are now."

"Most are in private hands, you know."

"Yes, I did know, but I would like to have the list."

"It's somewhat irregular. I don't know what the privacy concerns might be."

"I can't see that those who bought his paintings would be ashamed to have known that they did so."

"I don't know." He stroked his beard in an annoyingly narcissistic manner. "I don't know."

"Look. I can advise Mr. Bland to find someone in the private sector to do the cleaning and we can decide how we will proceed from there. Maybe a private gallery would be happy to dispose of the paintings."

"Now hang on a minute!" he barked. "There's no need to take that attitude. I'll put it to the Director. I think it will be alright."

"And the list?"

"I'll get you a copy right away."

I do not often whistle, but as I walked back to the Bugatti I must have sounded like a sparrow in springtime.

8

When I awoke the next day, I left early to meet a fisherman who would sell me some fresh mackerel, something which was almost impossible to obtain these days. On my way back to Grand Pre, I suddenly realized that I had failed to tell Rosalie of my plan to visit Paradise.

She came into the kitchen while I was baking some bread and starting to cook the fish. I asked her if she was amenable to a westward trip down the Valley, but I discovered that she had made plans to have lunch with Rachel.

"I can put off the Paradise visit to another day," I offered.

"No, that's fine. You go. I don't imagine you'll find anything of consequence. It's almost 75 years since he lived there—80 years since he arrived."

"You're probably right, but I feel I have to check it out."

"God," she said, "that mackerel smells delicious. Are you cooking it in butter?"

"A mixture of butter and olive oil."

"And is that bread I smell?"

"Yes, it should be about ready. Could you take it out of the oven?"

We had one of the best breakfasts in ages. We both love fish of all descriptions, and we absolutely adore mackerel. With a little salt and pepper it was outstanding, and the bread was a perfect accompaniment.

With the food, we tried out some Finca El Injerto coffee, which had very recently arrived in the mail from my specialty dealer in Toronto. Grown in Guatemala, the beans are rare, small and rich, and make a sumptuous brew. We both loved it, almost as much as our regular Jamaican Blue Mountain, and we agreed I should order more.

"Is there any particular reason why you're lunching with Rachel?" I asked.

"Yes. I find her a fascinating woman. I'm interested to find out more about her background. Partly because of professional interest and partly because she has no trouble putting you in your place!" She gave her wonderful, singing laugh.

"Yes, I admit she made a bit of a fool of me. But next time I'll make sure I know what I'm talking about."

"What time are you leaving?"

"I thought I'd go right after I've cleaned up the breakfast things. It's less than an hour each way on the 101. I could be back in time to join you for lunch."

"No," Rosalie said firmly, "don't do that. You'll only get into another argument. Besides, I think she could become a really good friend."

"You want to bond?"

"In a sense, yes. I'll keep you apprised of everything I find out."

"Fair enough. I might make a detour to Fulton's farm on the way back and see if I can get a few guinea fowl for dinner."

"Ooh. That would be lovely."

"I might cook some for you, if you play your cards right," I said, rising from the table.

"What do you mean?"

"You have to do the dishes! Bye!"

"Brute!"

There was very little traffic on the highway and the Bugatti went like a dream. This car was a complete joy to drive and, despite the

53

enormous inconvenience and expense, I was glad I had it shipped from England when I had returned to Nova Scotia about a year ago.

I was in Paradise in just over forty minutes. I took the 101 to the further exit and came back through the village from the western end.

On a fine day, Paradise is a lovely, sleepy village, the houses being set on either side of the main road with three or four side streets. Almost all of the houses were large and prosperous-looking, and a few were the very big, old places for which the Annapolis Valley is known.

I stopped at Pearle's Take-Out and asked the woman behind the counter if she knew of any very old residents. She offered a few names, but it became clear that they had been born long after Bland had left the community. She told me to try the Post Office, which she said was half a kilometre to the east on the left hand side. I thanked her, and slowly eased the Bugatti along the road.

I was almost into Lawrencetown before I realized that I must have missed the Post Office. So I turned off on Elliot Street and circled around in the entrance to the Community College Geographic Sciences campus, then back on to the road.

I drove even more slowly this time until I saw a house set back from the road with a Canada Post sign and mailbox. I drove past and parked alongside a beautiful, old, two-toned church, and walked back.

The Post Mistress was most obliging, telling me that the village's oldest resident was a Hattie Ingraham, who lived alone in a small house just across the street. She said she thought Hattie was about 96, maybe more. I asked if she was in good health and alert and was assured that she was still "as smart as a whip."

I asked her if she would do me a favour and call Hattie to see if it would be alright to visit her. She agreed, went into another room to phone, and came back with the information that Hattie would be "delighted to see me because she doesn't get many visitors, but she'll probably talk your ear off."

Mrs. Ingraham turned out to be charming old lady, very tiny and plump, with bright red apple cheeks, a winning smile and a twinkle in her bright blue eyes. She bustled about moving cushions and adjusting ornaments on various pieces of furniture, as she led me into a spotless, but clearly antiquated, kitchen. I guessed that very little had changed here in the past 50 years.

"Now, young man," she said in a high, but strong, voice with a country accent. "How can I help you?"

"Thank you so much, Mrs. Ingraham. Have you lived in Paradise all your life?"

"Yes apart from a few years at Normal College."

"When was that?"

"1949 I went to Truro on the Dominion Atlantic. But I didn't like it much. I only stayed there until Arthur popped the question."

"Arthur?"

"My late husband. He died years ago, God rest his soul."

"So, you would have been here in Paradise in 1943?"

"Yes. I was here all through the war."

"Mrs. Ingraham, do you remember Dr. John Bland?"

I was not prepared for the outburst which came from her. Her eyes widened and she blew out her cheeks with a snort.

"Indeed I do! A right smarmy sort, he was. I never trusted him, though sometimes when I were sick I didn't have no choice but to see him."

"Do you recall when he first arrived?"

"Yes. I would have been about 15 or 16 at the time. I remember he boarded with old Mrs. Isley up the road until he got married and bought a house. It's not there anymore. They knocked it down when they had to widen the road some years back."

"So, that was the first place he lived, at Mrs Isley's?"

"Well, there was talk he stayed with Herman Hempel for a day or two, but I never saw him there."

"Herman Hempel?"

"He was an old curmudgeon what got put away in the first war. I believe they sent him to Amherst. See, according to the law in them days, anyone who came to Canada—after 1902, I think it was—was judged to be an enemy alien."

"And this Herman Hempel came after 1902?"

"I guess so. He came here from Lunenburg in the 1930s. I don't know where he was before that."

"And when did Bland start his medical practice in Paradise?"

"Well, he come here for a little while, then he disappeared for a week or two—to Halifax, I think—and then he come back. 'Course he didn't go doctoring on his own right away. For a while he was an assistant to old Dr. Henry."

"Dr. Henry?"

"Henry Wilkinson. A fine old gentleman he were, and a good doctor too. I would always see him if I had the choice."

"What happened to Dr. Henry? Did he die?"

"I guess he did!" The old lady cackled. "If he didn't he would have been the only one of God's creatures as didn't!"

"No, I mean did he die here?"

"No, my love. He went off to the Carrybeen. Bermuda, I think."

"So how long, after he started with Dr. Henry, did Bland set up on his own?"

"Let me see….I think it were about two or three years. It were after he got married."

"And her name was Ida Murchison?"

"That's right. You already knew that. Imagine! Yes, Ida."

"What can you tell me about her, Mrs. Ingraham?"

"She was a strange one. Bit of an ugly duckling, but I got along with her alright. Nice enough in her own way. 'Course she had a sad time growing up."

"How so?"

"Well, there was five of them—apart from Mr. and Mrs. Murchison—and two of them, maybe three, I can't recall exactly, got that disease."

"What was it? Do you know what it was called?"

"Lord! Something like Porgy's disease, I think."

"Porgy's disease? How did it affect the children?"

"Well, it made them old before their time, didn't it? Very sad to see young children looking like old women. Like me!" She cackled again loudly, then wiped her eyes. "I shouldn't joke about such things, I know. Anyhow, they died."

"How old were they when they died?"

"Oh, about twelve, thirteen, I should say. I don't rightly know."

"Were they both girls?"

"I think so. Yes, at least two of them were. If there was a third I can't remember if it was a boy or girl."

"How did Bland and Ida meet?"

"Don't know. Maybe at church."

"Was their courtship very long?"

"No. Now I do know that. It was like he met and married her just like that. What a surprise, I can tell you!"

"Why?"

"Well, she was this dowdy, flat-chested, little thing from a very poor home and he was a young doctor, tall, blond and handsome."

"Good-looking, was he?"

"Some might say so. He was for sure striking. What they call athletic, except for his leg, of course."

"What was wrong with his leg?"

"He walked with a limp. Otherwise he would have been in the army, wouldn't he?"

"I'm not sure. I think perhaps doctors could get an exemption."

Jeremy Akerman

"Is that so? Anyways, I figured that the limp was there only when it suited him."

"You really didn't like him, did you?

"He was too full of himself for my liking."

"Arrogant?"

"Yes, that's the word. And, like I say, smarmy."

"Arrogant and smarmy. No wonder he wasn't popular."

"No, that was just me. I didn't like him one bit, but the rest of the village thought the sun shone out of his...well, you know what I mean." She looked at me for a minute and then loudly exclaimed, "Oh, my Lord!"

"What is it, Mrs. Ingraham?"

"I never offered you a cup of tea. What must you think of me?"

"That's okay. It's not necessary."

"No, no, no." She said bobbing up. "Now you wait there. I'll pop the kettle on and it'll be ready in no time. Meantime, you have a nice big piece of this."

She pushed a huge slab of remarkably-good-looking fruit cake towards me. It was almost black with fruit.

I cut off a small piece and tried it. "This is excellent," I said, "Did you buy it locally?"

"Buy it! I guess not! I made it myself," she declared proudly "Go on, have another piece. Now let me ask you something. Are you one of them as likes nice tea fresh from the pot, or are you like the ones around here who like it after it's stewed for a half hour?"

Since I was not sure what would be the correct answer, I was glad to have my mouth of cake.

"No, I can see you're one of the sensible ones. Fresh tea it is then."

I nodded vigorously as I watched her pour the tea into delicately decorated china cups which looked as if they had been with her for three quarters of a century.

"How long was Dr. Bland in Paradise, Mrs. Ingraham?"

"About five or maybe six years, I reckon. I was glad to see him go."

"And now I have to go, Mrs. Ingraham. Thank you so very, very much for your help."

"You're welcome. Are you going to write a book or something?"

"No, I'm just making inquiries on behalf of his grandson."

"Hmph! Well, I hope he's nothing like his grandfather was."

"No, he isn't. He's a fine man."

"I'm glad to hear it. Now, goodbye young man, I have to get ready for my television program. I like that Dr. Phil."

Jeremy Akerman

9

When I returned from my trip to Paradise, there was a message from Rosalie on the answering machine. She said that she and Rachel were getting along so well, and that the story of Rachel's background was so absorbing, that they were going to spend the rest of the day together.

So, I put the guinea fowl I had bought at Fulton's farm in the fridge and made myself a cold collation for dinner. Searching around, I found some Bayonne ham, part of a chicken, two tomatoes, some celery and a chunk of Beaufort cheese. To accompany this I opened a bottle of Louis-Benjamin-Didier Dagueneau Pouilly Fumé Asteroid, from the Loire.

I ate at my desk and, while I was munching, I googled Porgy's disease and got a bunch of information about fish! Then I entered premature aging and came up with a disease called progeria.

It was a rare genetic condition which caused rapid aging in children. A tiny genetic mutation caused the disease and resulted in signs of aging such as balding and wrinkled skin. I noted that the condition was always fatal.

Progeria was first described by Dr. Jonathan Hutchinson and Dr. Hastings Gilford in the late 1800s. They found that the average age of death was 14 years, although some adults with progeria did live into their early 20s. Death most often occurred as a result of complications of severe atherosclerosis.

After dining, I called Ray. "Hi, Ray. I've lost my wife. Do you know where she is?"

"Hello, Marc. I'm in the same boat as you. I have no idea where they are."

"I guess they'll show up eventually. I went to Paradise today."

"How did you make out?"

"Not bad. It seems your grandfather was a real charmer, but those who didn't fall for his charm really disliked him."

"Like my mother. And maybe my dad, too, but he wouldn't discuss his old man."

"The most interesting thing I discovered was that, while he was considered a handsome catch, your grandmother was plain and drab."

"Really?"

"The old lady I talked to said she was 'a dowdy, flat chested little thing.' Apparently, their marriage came as a huge surprise to the locals. It would seem he met her and wed here in no time flat."

"I never met her, or even saw a photo of her."

"I was told that at least two of her sisters had progeria."

"What's that?"

"That's the name of the premature aging disease."

"Nasty."

"Yes."

"That all?"

"Pretty much."

"My neighbour is coming back from vacation. So we can have a crack at the strongbox."

"Good. When?"

"Day after tomorrow. Have you thought any more about the safe?"

"I'll go to New Minas tomorrow and see if my locksmith friend has any ideas."

"Okay, Marc. Thanks for giving me an update."

I went back to learning more about progeria. The literature told me that the symptoms include growth failure, short stature, tough and wrinkled skin, balding, stiff joints with decreased range of motion, and loss of body fat. Also, strange things happen to the head and face, including a large, open, soft spot on the head, a narrow face for the size of the head, a beaked nose, and a small, underdeveloped jaw. Later, there could be hip dislocation, cataracts, arthritis, and plaque buildup in the arteries.

It was impossible to prevent progeria because it was due to a new genetic mutation, which meant it happened randomly. The condition typically didn't run in families, which made it difficult to predict. However, if someone had a child with progeria, the chances of having another child with the disease did increase.

I gathered that the rarity of a parent passing on the disease was only established later in the 20th century. So the chances of it occurring in siblings in Ida's family and it reappearing in her own children would have been something like ten thousand to one, but nobody would have known that at the time.

I shut down the computer, poured myself a glass of 18-year-old Abelour single malt, and put on a recording of Mahler's 2nd, the so-called "resurrection symphony."

This turned out to be a huge mistake, as the music was so dramatic and exciting that when I went to bed, my mind was full of jumbled visions of Christ on the cross and stunted children with wrinkles and beaked noses.

10

When I awoke, Rosalie was lying beside me, but I had not heard her come to bed so I did not know how late it was when she arrived home.

I crept out of bed as quietly as I could so as not to disturb her, and came down to the kitchen to see what we had on hand for breakfast. We had not done our grocery shopping that week, so the pickings were lean: half a box of eggs, an onion, five or six mushrooms, half a carton of cream, a rather pathetic-looking green pepper, the ends of four different cheeses and the remainder of the Bayonne ham.

There was only one thing to be done, and that was to make a frittata.

I finely chopped the onions and the green pepper, sliced the mushrooms, carved the ham into small strips and grated the cheese. Then I whipped the eggs and cream, tipped in all the other ingredients and poured everything into an ovenproof dish.

I figured it would take about forty minutes at 375 to cook, after which it would need a further ten minutes resting. By that time I guessed Rosalie would be rousing.

She came down almost exactly as the frittata was ready to eat, when the coffee was perking steadily and the croissants were hot from my other oven.

"Something smells good," she said, stretching.

"What time did you get in?"

"After midnight. Rachel is quite a talker when she gets going."

"Must have been. You were gone a long time. Where did you have dinner?"

"Li's. It was quite good."

"Yes, I've heard that Jewish people like Chinese food."

"I think that's stereotyping. But I understand that on Christmas Day they like to go Chinese."

"Sit yourself down while I serve up. Then I want a full report."

"Fair enough. Afterwards I want a report on Paradise."

"It's a deal."

I laid the frittata on a table mat and cut it into manageable-sized chunks, then laid out the croissants and the butter and poured the coffee. We were both hungry and waded into the frittata with gusto.

Later, as I was putting some English marmalade on a croissant, Rosalie drained her coffee cup and took a notebook from her purse.

"You kept notes? Of a conversation? My God, what did Rachel think of that?"

"She knows I am a professional historian, so she told me to go ahead and take all the notes I wanted. Besides, she said I would never remember the names if I didn't."

"Well, it should make for a thorough record of your day."

"Her paternal grandparents came from a place called Bucha. Their family had been in Ukraine for hundreds of years, during which there had been a thriving Jewish community. Rachel told me that much of modern Hebrew and Yiddish culture originated in Ukraine. She mentioned several people I'd never heard of."

"Who were they?"

"Let me see...Haim Bialik, a famous poet, was one, and Isaac Levisohn was another. And someone I had heard of was Sholom Aleichem, the man who created Tvye who we know from *Fiddler on the Roof.*"

"What were the grandparents' names?"

"Abramsky. Ulen and Zhanna Abramsky."

"And they were the ones who were murdered by the Nazis?"

"Yes. The same as in Russia and elsewhere, there had been anti-Semitism in Ukraine long before the Nazis arrived. There were violent pogroms against the Jews in the 19th Century and into the 20th. But by the time of the Second World War Ukraine had the biggest Jewish population in Europe."

"I didn't know that."

"Neither did I. Apparently, there were close to three million Jews there."

"What percentage of the total population would that have been?"

"About five percent."

"And I guess the anti-Semites in Ukraine welcomed the Nazis with open arms?"

"More or less, but Rachel was at great pains to point out that they were a very small share of the populace. She said that most people have no idea that the Germans killed more Ukrainians than the people they killed in any other country."

"Really? I had no idea."

"It was a staggering number. Military losses alone were over four million people and another six million Ukrainians died in Nazi-occupied Ukraine. 1.5 million of them were Jews."

"Wow!"

"She also told me that 4.5 million Ukrainians fought against the Nazis as members of the Red Army."

"Were Ukrainian losses counted as part of Russia's war losses, or were they separate?"

"No, Ukrainians represented as much as 35% of all Russian dead."

"Amazing! So, when was Rachel's dad born?"

"He was born in 1940. His name was Saul."

"But if his parents were killed at Babi Yar in 1941, what happened to Saul?"

"He was brought up by his grandmother. Fortunately for him, she lived long enough to see him grow into a man."

"What did he do?"

"He was a farm supervisor. He made Aliyah in 1958."

"Aliyah? What's that?"

"That means going up, or moving to Israel."

"Fascinating stuff. What about Rachel's mother's parents? Where did they come from?"

"They came as kids with their parents to what was then Palestine from Russia in 1919, just after World War One. Apparently, they took a look at the Communists who had taken over in Russia late in 1917, and decided they were no better than the Germans."

"And what were the names of her grandparents?"

"Rivkin. Mendel and Sarra."

"Where did Rachel get the name King?"

"Rachel says she was briefly married to Mr. King years ago."

"Oh. That would explain it."

"Rachel's mom, Klara, was born in 1952. But before that it seems Mendel and Sarra really went through the meat grinder."

"How so?"

"It's a gruesome story. Wherever they went, it seems they always happened to be in the wrong place at the wrong time. Shortly after they arrived in the Middle East, in 1921, their parents moved the family to Jaffa just before the Arabs rioted and killed over 40 Jews and injured around 140. Later, they moved to Hebron, but in 1929 there was another Arab revolt over their claim to the sanctity of the Al-Aqsa Mosque in Jerusalem."

"Wait a minute! What was their problem?"

"Who?"

"The Arabs."

"There was a rumour the Jews were going to seize the Temple Mount, where the mosque is."

"And were they?"

"No, the rumour was groundless and may have been started by the Mufti of Jerusalem, who encouraged the mob."

"Who was he?"

"He was Haj Amin Al Husseini. A lovely guy who later allied himself with Hitler and raised Muslim regiments for the Nazis."

"Hold on. I'm confused. Why did this guy think the rumour would stick?"

"Because the Jews' Western Wall, a remnant of the Second Temple, is located there. It is the most holy site in Judaism."

"When was that temple built?"

"Give or take, somewhere between 600 BC and 60 AD."

"And when was the mosque built?"

"In 1035."

"So the Jews were there first?"

"By a long shot. The Umayyad caliph Abd al-Malik built his mosque on top of the temple site."

"No wonder the site evokes strong feelings! Is there any coffee left in the pot?"

Rosalie put aside her notes and went to the counter, coming back with the pot. There was just enough for two not very full cups.

"So, we have Mendel and Sarra in Hebron when this is all kicking off. What happened there?"

"The Arabs slaughtered around seventy Jews and burned down their synagogues and houses. In Safed, where one of their relatives lived, eighteen Jews were killed, forty wounded and around two

Jeremy Akerman

hundred houses were looted and burned."

"But they survived?

"Yes. And somewhere along the line, Saul met the Rivkins and fell for Klara. They were married in 1980. He was 40 and she was 28. Rachel was born ten years later."

"How did she get to Canada?"

"By air, I should imagine." She laughed.

"No silly. You know what I mean!"

"She came to go to McGill, and when she had completed her post graduate degree, she met Mr. King and the rest in history."

"That was quite a story, Rosalie. Thanks. Rachel sounds like a remarkable woman."

"She is. Ray's a very lucky man. Now tell me all about Paradise."

"I will, but it's small potatoes compared with your report."

11

The next morning I drove the Bugatti to New Minas to see the locksmith about the safe in Ray's attic. As I was passing Greenwich I heard a slight ticking coming from the engine. Nothing lit up on the dash or registered on any of the gauges, so I put it out of my mind, dismissing it as something I had picked up on a tire.

When I got to the locksmith's, I gave him the notes we had made from the front of the safe. He examined them carefully then consulted several manuals.

"I've not had personal experience with this type. It's an old model, but built like Fort Knox. There's no way I know of that will get us in via the tumblers and relock."

"How could we get in?"

"A thermic lance would do it in no time, but I've no idea where we would get one of those. We'd have to use an oxy acetylene cutter."

"Do you have such a thing?"

"No, but I could easily borrow one from Albert at the garage down the street."

"Great!"

"Not so fast. Where is this safe?"

"In Ray's attic."

"Can't use oxy acetylene there. People could suffocate from the fumes and we could start a fire. Can we move it outside, or at least into a well-ventilated area?"

"Only by knocking a hole in a wall or the roof. Then we'd have the problem of getting it to the ground from three floors up."

"How high is it?"

"I'm guessing about seven and a half metres."

"Then you'll need a crane. A Carry Deck 2.5 tonner should do it."

"Can you get one?"

"Sure. I can get one from my wife's cousin, Willy. But it'll cost you."

"How much?"

"Couldn't say. But it would be in the hundreds, for sure. Maybe a grand. Let me talk to him and I'll see what I can do to beat him down."

"Okay, thanks. Do you know a reliable builder who could make an entrance way into the attic?"

"You'd need the crane to do that. My brother George could do it. If we started early in the day, we could make the hole, drag out the safe, bring her to the ground, go to work with the oxyacetylene, and get her open by supper time."

"How about patching up the hole properly?"

"Have to come back the next day for that."

"But it could all be done?"

"Sure."

"Alright. Would you set that up for me?"

"Yep. Might take some time. To pull all the elements together could be a couple of weeks."

"Do your best and let me know."

As I was heading back to Grand Pre, I heard the ticking again so I thought I would drive directly to Halifax and have my mechanic, Liam Candow, take a look at it. So, I headed for the 101 and got into the city in an hour and a half.

I left the car in Liam's capable hands and, since it was a lovely day, called a cab to take me downtown to the Public Gardens, which I had not seen for a few years.

The gardens were lush and green, and I was glad to see that several of the older, grander trees had managed to survive the hideous vandalism which some malevolent miscreants had perpetrated upon them in 2022. There was a magnificent display of flowers to be seen in various locations, my favourites being the long beds which contained as many as 30 varieties planted in an almost random fashion.

The large trees, some of them planted 150 years ago, sheltered the gardens from the wind, so it was very warm inside. I took off my jacket, sat on a bench and closed my eyes, enjoying the heat of the sun on my face.

I must have fallen asleep because I was awakened by a voice calling to me.

"Mr. LeBlanc? Marc LeBlanc?"

I squinted into the sun and could just make out an upright, elderly man standing in front of me. After a few seconds I was able to see that it was someone I had met the previous year when I was investigating the Holy Grail matter. He had been an archaeologist at the Fortress of Louisbourg in the 1960s and I had consulted him about one of his excavations.

"Mr. Akerman. How are you? Please sit down."

"Thank you. I thought it was you. What brings you to the city? You live in Wolfville, don't you?"

"Grand Pre, actually."

"Ah yes. I learned the reason for your coming to see me last year from the newspapers. And I heard about the denouement of the affair."

"Ah yes. It was briefly in the news."

"If I may say so, I think your ultimate decision was a wise one."

"Thank you. Not everyone thinks as you do."

"On serious matters," said Akerman, "unanimity is impossible to achieve."

"Indeed."

"Did your experience with the Grail cure you of the inclination towards detective work, or did it spur you on to greater mysteries?"

"As a matter of fact, the latter. I'm currently in the middle of a mystery which is proving as difficult as it is fascinating."

"Do tell. I should like to hear about it."

"It involves the grandfather of a friend of mine. He knows almost nothing about the older man, but feels he must find out because his Granddad was so mysterious."

"Mysterious, in what way?"

"He appeared out of nowhere in the Annapolis Valley around 1942, became a doctor and subsequently a fairly respected landscape painter."

"Where was this?"

"I said, in the Annapolis Valley."

"Yes, yes, but where in the Annapolis Valley?"

"A little place called Paradise."

"Paradise? Is that anywhere near St. Croix Cove?"

"I don't know."

"Do you have a map on you?"

"No."

"I don't use mobile phones. But if you have one you could look it up."

"Why? Is it important?"

"It could be."

It took me a few minutes to bring up a map of Nova Scotia on my phone, then zoom into part of it where Paradise was shown. I looked around until I found St. Croix Cove.

"Yes it is. It's about 10 kilometres away."

"You'd better tell me the whole story," Akerman said. "Then I'll tell you why I was asking."

So, I related everything I knew and everything we had found out, from being first asked by Ray to take the case to what I had learned two days ago.

His eyes brightened and a smile played around his lips. "Remarkable," he said.

"Why? What is remarkable?"

"About twenty-five years ago I used to do mystery weekends at different country hotels. I would use a handful of actors and base my plot on some story or legend connected with the area in which the particular inn was located."

"Yes?"

"Well, one of them where I put on these mystery weekends was the Blomidon Inn in Wolfville."

"I'm sorry, Mr. Akerman. But I don't see the connection."

"You will. One of these plots I based on something I learned from obscure military records. It was that in 1942 a German U-boat, *Der Feinste*, was observed coming into the Bay of Fundy."

"Let me guess," I said. "This U-boat went to St. Croix Cove."

"Bingo!" Akerman said. "She was observed coming close to shore, not for very long, just long enough to launch a dinghy. But do you know what was particular about it?"

"What"

"The man who saw it said three people came ashore in the dinghy, but only two went back."

The hair stood up on the back of my neck and a chill ran right through me. My mouth was dry, so I had difficulty speaking. "Holy cow! You mean that whoever didn't go back to the submarine could have been Ray's grandfather?"

"Exactly."

"It fits. It makes sense."

"Yes, but you have no way of proving it."

Jeremy Akerman

"I think we might," I said, thinking of the strong box we would open tomorrow. "I just think we might."

I called Liam to see if the car was ready, but he said he needed to do another test in the morning and I could pick it up around eleven. So, after thanking Akerman, I called Rosalie, wandered around the city and checked into the Muir Hotel.

Later, I had dinner at Café Lunette where the food was good but the place was very noisy. I went to bed early, thinking that at last we had a break in the case!

12

Ray called me the next morning, informing me that if we went to his house that evening after dinner, his neighbour, Bill, would open the strong box.

I did not tell Rosalie about the *Feinste* coming to St. Croix Cove in 1942. I was not sure why, but I think I didn't want to alarm anyone without having further proof. I thought that in the absence of additional evidence I would keep it from Ray and Rachel indefinitely, telling Rosalie only when the whole business was over. If the connection was established, I imagine it would be particularly unpleasant to Rachel.

We arrived at Port Williams around seven-thirty and were introduced to Bill Hartley, who was a round, cheerful man in his forties. He wore overalls and carried a heavy cut-off saw, a large bag and a length of cable.

We all trooped up to the attic, Ray leading. When we entered and turned on the swinging light, Bill shuffled around the walls, moving boxes and bundles.

"What's up Bill?" Ray asked.

"No power outlet. I can't see one."

"Damn. I guess there aren't any. Can you run your cable from the bedroom on the next floor down?"

"I'll give it a try, but it doesn't look long enough."

Ray took the end of the cable and hurried downstairs.

"Any luck?"

"No. It'll only reach just inside the door."

"Okay. I'll nip next door and get an extension." Bill rattled down the stairs and out of the house.

Rachel pulled me to one side. "Marc, I would like a word with you a little later."

"Sure. What about?"

"The other night I got the impression that you thought my accusations of bias against the media was some kind of conspiracy theory."

"Oh, I wouldn't say that."

"But you were skeptical?"

"Somewhat. The charge seemed a little sweeping."

"I can see how you might think that. If we get a chance in a little while, come down to the kitchen. I have something to show you."

"Okay. I'd be glad to."

"Thanks." Rachel said. "Here's Bill with his extension."

Bill plugged one cable into the bedroom outlet, came out onto the landing and connected the extension, then came back to the attic. He plugged in his equipment, unscrewed the bolt, inserted a diamond, steel-cutting blade, aligned it to the arrows on the saw and tightened the bolt with a wrench. He took a pair of goggles and put them on, extracted a large pair of industrial safety earmuffs from his bag, then put on a mask.

"I figure the best thing is to take a lid off by cutting about two inches from the top. That way we won't damage anything inside."

"Sounds good. Go ahead, Bill."

"You won't want to stick around," said Bill. "The noise and the dust will be something awful."

"Okay," said Ray. "Everybody downstairs until Bill calls us to come back up."

When we were on the second floor, the intense whining of the saw started. It reminded me of the sound made by Stukas in newsreels from World War II, and we hurried on down.

When we were in the kitchen, Rachel called me over to a large sideboard where she had laid out some papers on which headlines from various news outlets had been tagged with the publication or network and the date. The sources varied from the CBC, BBC, *New York Times*, Al Jazeera, *Washington Post*, CNN, *The Guardian*, *The Daily Mail*, CBS and others.

"I want you to look at these, one by one, Marc, and tell me what is going on in each of them."

The first said

TelAviv shooting. Three killed in shopping centre

and the second said

Shooting incident kills three

"I guess some wacko shot three people," I said lamely.

"No. An armed Arabs terrorist opened fire and gunned down three Israeli citizens. Read the next."

Two Palestinians killed as daily violence continues

"I don't know. It sounds as if the army or the police shot them."

"Yes, but only after the 'Palestinians" charged at a police officer with machetes. Read the next."

Six dead in Jerusalem

"It could be anything, I guess."

"But it wasn't just anything. Four of the dead were Israeli civilians and the other two were Arab terrorists who killed them in a synagogue, and were then shot by police. Read this from CNN describing the same incident."

Deadly attack on Jerusalem mosque

"You're joking. They changed the synagogue to mosque?"
"They did. How about this one?"

Palestinian shot dead in Jerusalem. Two Israelis also killed

"Someone, we don't know who, shot three people. It happens."
"No." Rachel said. "The 'Palestinian' was an armed terrorist who killed three Israelis and then was shot by police."

Jordan slams Israel after radical Jews visit Islamic holy site

"That's self-explanatory."
"Is it? The 'Islamic holy site' referred to is the Temple Mount, which has been Judaism's holiest site for well over a thousand years and where the Jews built two temples. As you can see, I have many, many more examples. But just two more, then I'll let you go."

Israeli raid kills five Palestinians

"I imagine this was a raid by the army. I don't know why."
"It was a raid by police after armed Arab terrorists were carrying bombs to explode in civilian areas. Last one."

Israel unrest. Boy, 16, becomes seventh Palestinian killed by security forces after Jerusalem stabbings as wave of violence continues.

"First," Rachel said, "the 'wave of violence' was an intifada launched by the Arabs in which a number of Israelis were killed. Second, the 'boy' was an Arab terrorist who stabbed several elderly Jewish men."

"I don't know what to say."

"But you now think I may have at least something of a point relative to media bias?"

"Yes, I do. It is all egregious, and some of it is outrageous. In one case, the network just invented the story."

"Now you have some idea what we are up against. Tell me it is not anti-Semitism and I'll call you a fool or a liar."

The whining stopped. Bill clattered downstairs, covered in dust. "You can go up in a minute or two. I've neatly taken the top off your strong box. Although I have no clue how you're going to get into that safe. It's a monster."

"What's inside, Bill?"

"Just a lot of old files and papers as far as I could see. I didn't look at them."

"What's your guess, Marc?" Rachel asked.

"They will be in German," I said without thinking.

"What?" They spoke at the same time.

"The documents will be in German. It's just a guess. If I'm right I'll tell you later why."

We clambered up the stairs and, stooping low, went into the attic, now smelling of metallic burning.

Ray went over to the strongbox, reached in, pulled out a file and opened it. "Damnit! Marc's right. It is in German!"

"Anybody speak the language?" Rachel asked with a shudder.

Nobody did, but Bill made a feeble joke by shouting, "Nein, Mein Fuhrer." Rachel shot him a glance of disgust.

"I think we need to hire a researcher," I said. "You know, like you were on the last caper, Rosalie, but this time one who is a fluent

German speaker."

"I'll inquire at the University tomorrow. I'm sure I can find someone."

"Marc!" Ray's voice was like steel.

"What is it, Ray?"

"You'll never guess what is at the bottom of the box, occupying the whole lower area."

"Let me try," I said very quietly so only he could hear. "Is it an old radio transmitter?"

"How the hell did you know?"

"I guessed."

I moved closer to Ray and, putting my back to the others, muttered to him that we should not discuss it any further with Bill present. He nodded.

"Well, I think that's enough mystery for one day," he said, standing up. "Thank you so much, Bill, you've been a great help. If we all go downstairs I have a bottle of rum for you as a token of our thanks."

"Gee, thanks, Ray." Bill was all smiles. "I must get back anyway. The wife will be wondering where I've got to."

He gathered up his tools and equipment and we helped him carry them down the stairs. When we reached the living room, Ray presented him with a bottle of Appleton Estate 15 year old rum.

"This is something special, Ray. Many thanks. Nice to meet you folks. I may see you again the next time you need a strong box broken into."

As soon as he had left and we saw him crossing the lawn to his own house, the others all turned on me, demanding answers.

"I think it fairly probable that Ray's grandfather was a member of the Nazi *Abwehr* who was landed here from a U-boat called the *Feinste* late in 1942. I think, when we hire our assistant and translate the contents of the strong box, we'll find some kind of confirmation. Sorry, Ray. Sorry, Rachel."

"Darling," Ray said to her, "I hope this doesn't make any difference to us."

"Of course not, you idiot! Just because your grandfather may have been a Nazi doesn't make you more than a Brownshirt."

Ray's face fell in dismay, but Rachel's peal of laughter soon brought a smile back to his face. They embraced so passionately that Rosalie and I felt embarrassed, so we hastily made our excuses and headed out.

"We can resume discussion of this tomorrow night," I said. "Come to dinner. We can recap and then see where we go from here."

"Yes," said Rosalie. "We're having guinea fowl. Come about six thirty."

13

Early the following day I received a call from Louise LeBlanc, informing me that she had acquired a spacious storefront on Main Street, had it outfitted appropriately, had obtained all necessary licenses and permits, and was now ready to acquire inventory. Depending upon how long enough stock would take to arrive, she reckoned that we might be able to open the wine store in three to five months.

She wanted to consult with me on the types and origins of the products we should offer, so I agreed to go and see her at ten o'clock.

Over a scrumptious breakfast of eggs Benedict with mushrooms and lashings of Blue Mountain coffee, which Rosalie prepared, she told me that while she was at the university that morning she would approach a young graduate student who was fluent in German to help us with our research. This was the kind of role which Rosalie herself had occupied during our quest for the Holy Grail, and was how I first met her.

"Who is this person?" I asked.

"His name is Leslie Alsop. His specialty is German history of the twentieth century."

"Sounds like the very man we want."

"Yes, but I was wondering how much Ray would be prepared to pay him."

"How long would we need him, do you think?"

"Not as long as you needed me last time," she said with a laugh. "I'm guessing a month would be okay."

"What did I pay you?"

"Not enough! You'd have to pay him over the minimum wage—say the equivalent of $20 an hour—so I'd say about $3500 would do it."

"I'll call Ray right now and see what he says."

I got Ray just as he was leaving for work and put the proposition to him. He seemed a little reticent.

"What's the problem, Ray? Money?"

"No, no, not the money. Would this person be sworn to secrecy? I don't want some stranger washing my family's dirty linen all over the place."

"We could insist on that as one of the terms of employment. But it may cost us more."

"None of us can speak a word of German, so we need someone."

"And someone who not only speaks the language, but is capable of doing research in German, too."

"Okay. Tell Rosalie to drive the best bargain she can."

"If she can get a good deal, we should ask him to give us a preliminary report...when?"

"How about Saturday?"

"Got it. Now, how can he get the contents of the strongbox?"

"Why doesn't Rosalie ask him to have lunch with us at Li's and I'll bring the stuff with me?"

"Twelve thirty?"

"Fine."

I arrived at the address Louise had given me on time, and found a space to park the Bugatti. She greeted me on the sidewalk, obviously pleased that our project was finally coming to fruition.

We went inside and immediately I could see she had done an outstanding job, not only attending to every detail of the logistics of a wine store, but achieving a remarkably beautiful ambience.

I decided on the spot to make her a partner in the enterprise, at no cost to her, because I reasoned that if she had a 49% ownership she would be even more diligent. She was thrilled when I told her and her face lit up.

I had not known her for long, and had forgotten how we had become acquainted, but I had been impressed with her business-like manner and commonsense. She looked like a caricature of an accountant: stiff, upright, and efficient, complete with a white blouse, horn-rimmed spectacles and her hair in a bun. Suppliers and customers alike would understand that, while she would be scrupulously fair and honest, she would take no nonsense from them.

The shop was not particularly wide, so the storefront was only of average size, but the premises were deep, well over 100 feet, with the last 25 feet being somewhat narrower than the rest. We agreed that the smaller space should be temperature-controlled and that we should keep our special, more expensive products there, displaying our more reasonably-priced wines in the larger front section.

"Do you agree that we should not just copy other stores and have a little of just about everything on earth?" I asked.

"Absolutely, Marc. I think we should decide on maybe a dozen areas—not countries—and represent them well."

"Exactly what I had in mind. First, we must decide what we won't carry. For instance, I think carrying Bordeaux is crazy. It's phenomenally expensive and takes decades to be ready to drink."

"Right. Same with Burgundy. That is the Côte de Beaune and Côtes des Nuits. Too expensive, and unreliable. We should stock good Beaujolais and the best of the Chalonnais."

"Agreed. Are Napa and Sonoma out?"

"I think so, unless we get a great deal on something. In California, let's go for Santa Maria Valley and the Santa Cruz Mountains.

In Spain, let's have the Ribera de Duero."

"Makes sense. How about Italy? There's a lot to choose from."

"One thing is for sure," said Louise. "We won't carry seventeen brands of Pinot Grigio, the way the Liquor Corporation does. That's absolutely nuts!"

"Agreed!"

We went on in this manner for several hours, choosing lesser-known areas which produced high quality wines. The part of the shop nearest the window we would reserve for really good Nova Scotia wines, which we reckoned amounted to about 15% of the province's production. We were resolved that if customers wanted "plonk" to have a cheap drunk, they could go somewhere else.

Louise and I became so absorbed in our wine selection that I was late getting to Li's.

I peeked in the window and saw Ray, Rosalie and a young man at a corner table. Ray was pushing files and notebooks across the table. Rachel was not present, presumably not being able to get away from the hospital.

Leslie Alsop was a tiny little fellow with a ridiculous ponytail, rings through his cheeks, a wispy beard, and tattoos on his neck. I hoped that his knowledge of German and his researching talents were more prepossessing than his appearance.

When I was seated, we got down to business. At first, Alsop balked at a secrecy agreement, but gave in when Ray upped the offer to $3800 for the month.

"You'll only get half of that up front," Ray said. "And we'll have Walter Bryden draw up something you will need to sign."

"Why all the heavy security, man?" Alsop asked.

"It's no big deal. It's just that we may discover some unpleasant facts about my grandfather, which I would rather not have bandied about the county."

"That's fair enough, I guess."

"So you agree?"

"Yeah. Do you want me to look through this stuff right away?"

"We'd like you to give us a preliminary report on Saturday," I said. "Would that be alright?"

"Sure. I can do that. Where?"

"Port Williams. My place," said Ray.

"I got no car. You'll have to pick me up."

"Okay."

"And take me back after."

"Marc and I'll do that," Rosalie said.

Alsop shovelled all the files, papers and notebooks into a voluminous backpack, got up and unceremoniously shuffled out of the restaurant.

"Isn't he eating anything?" I asked.

"Apparently not," said Ray.

"Rosalie. What do you know about this character? I don't like the look of him."

"Marc, you know better than to judge a book by its cover. His marks have been astronomical ever since he came to Acadia some years ago. They say his theses have been topnotch, and his professors tell me he is absolutely brilliant."

"If Ray is happy with him, I'll go along with it."

"Let's see what we get on Saturday," Ray said. "If I'm not satisfied, then I'll pay him off."

"That sounds reasonable. You haven't forgotten you and Rachel are coming to dinner this evening?"

"No way. We want to know how you knew the stuff in the strong box would be in German."

That afternoon I chose the evening's menu carefully, having regard to Rachel's kosher requirements. Eventually I came up with a bouillabaisse-like soup (but without shellfish) to start, then guinea fowl poached in white wine with slices of truffle inserted under the skin for the main course, then crêpes Suzette for dessert.

With the soup I intended to serve my last bottle of Ridge Chardonnay 2003; with the guinea fowl, a Pommard, 1er Cru Clos des Epeneaux Comte Armand 2001; and with dessert à Chateau Rieussec 1998. Before the meal I thought we would have a bottle of Krug 1995.

First I made a fish stock with roughly-chopped vegetables; parsley; and bay leaf; and fish bones, heads and skin. Then I finely chopped two onions, two leeks, a carrot, a fennel root, and sautéed them gently in olive oil before adding a cup of white wine and four cups of the stock.

Into this I ground a spoonful of saffron and a small spring of thyme. I cut up pieces of salmon, haddock and cod, and put them on a plate to be added to the liquid only minutes before eating. A fresh baguette went into the oven to crisp.

In a giant pot I put some herbs and chopped onions, two bottles of dry Riesling and the two guinea fowl with their truffle additions (the French call it "in half mourning"), and poached them very gently until just before carving and serving. Normally I would serve the birds with a cream sauce, but, in deference to Rachel, I made a simple *beurre blanc* (made with Kosher butter) and intended to serve it with tiny potatoes.

Over the Krug, which turned out to be a little too rich for an aperitif, I related my experience with my former archaeologist friend in the Halifax public gardens.

"You'll remember him, Rosalie. He was the guy who excavated the L'Artigue house at Louisbourg."

"Yes, I do. Funny your running into him again."

"He was taking a stroll in the park and I was napping on a bench."

"What happened?"

"Well, he told me that some twenty-five years ago he did some research and found that a German U-boat, the *Feinste*, had sailed up the Bay of Fundy late in 1942 and was rumoured to have landed someone on the coast not that far from Paradise."

"Why?"

"I guess the person could have been a spy. Anyway, John Bland appeared in Paradise around the same time. So it fits."

"How would he be able to pass as a local?" Rachel asked.

"He wouldn't have had to pass as a local, just as a Canadian."

"How would he do that?"

"Maybe he had special coaching in American English. Maybe he had been to Canada before."

"Like on some kind of business?" Ray asked.

"Or on vacations," Rosalie suggested.

"Yes! That would be it, Rosalie," Rachel said.

"Maybe he had a relative here who he regularly visited?"

"An aunt, maybe."

"Maybe it was this Herman Hempel character Mrs. Ingraham told you about when you went to Paradise."

"Yes. It could be. That would make sense."

"But wouldn't Mrs. Ingraham have remembered a boy visiting Hempel from out of town?" Ray asked.

"She said Hempel came from Lunenburg," I said. "Perhaps John Bland visited him there. Anyway, let's eat. We can talk more when we are at the table."

Everybody moved into the dining room as I went to the kitchen, turned up the heat under the soup and, when it was really hot, dropped in the pieces of fish. I left them for no more than two minutes then took the pot off the stove and took it to the table.

While everybody was helping themselves to soup, I quickly cut the baguette into chunks and put them in a basket.

"Presumably, John Bland's visits took place before about 1920, when Hempel's World War One detention would have ended, and about 1935, when Hitler's aggressive intentions were becoming clear," Ray said.

It sounded strange his referring to his own grandfather as "John Bland", and I wondered if he was already starting to put distance between them, largely for Rachel's sake.

"How old was he when he died, Ray?" Rosalie asked.

"My parents said he was eighty."

"When did he die?"

"Nineteen ninety-five. I was seven at the time."

"Then he would have been born in 1915. It's not likely he would have done much transatlantic travelling before he was 15 or so, so his visits would have to have been squeezed into the period between 1930 and 1935."

"Turbulent years in Germany," said Rachel.

"Maybe that's why he was sent to Canada."

"We may find out on Saturday," I said. "Now, let's have that guinea fowl!"

Jeremy Akerman

14

When I awoke the next morning, Rosalie was not in the bed, and when I went downstairs I saw by the plates in the sink that she had already eaten breakfast. I poked my head into the living room and saw her at the desk, busy on the computer.

"You were up early."

"I couldn't sleep. I had something on my mind so I had to get up and work on it."

"What was it?"

"I'll tell you when I've cracked it. You go and eat. I'll be in soon with some news."

I was intrigued, but knew better than to press her before she was ready, so I made myself some smoked haddock poached in creamy milk, and two eggs cracked into the pan with the fish.

When the food was cooked, I slathered it with butter and ate it with thinly sliced bread and what is known as Geisha coffee from Hacienda La Esmeralda, on the slopes of Volcán Barú in Panama. I was just finishing up when Rosalie came in with a look of triumph on her beautiful face.

"So?"

"Seventh Canada census 1931, District of Queens-Lunenburg, sub-district New Germany West," she announced.

"Aha! Good girl. New Germany! You couldn't make it up."

"Isn't that priceless? Marc, did you know that the census asked 40 different questions in those days?"

"I didn't."

"Most of the answers are irrelevant for our purposes, but here we find Hempel, Hermann, age 40, farmer. Religion Lutheran."

"Fantastic! Any relatives?"

"None listed."

"Hmm. Anything else?"

"But of course. Eighth Canada Census 1941, district of Annapolis-Kings, sub-district Lawrencetown. Hempel, Hermann, age 50. Smallholder."

"Well done!"

"Did you know that Nova Scotia's population was only 578,000 in 1941?"

"No. That seems small."

"Yes, it does, considering we just passed a million last year."

"Rosalie, this means that John Bland—if he did come here before his mysterious arrival in 1942—must have visited Herman Hempel in the period from, say, 1930 to sometime before 1941. And, as we've already noted, it's likely it happened before 1935."

"Yes. How can we pin it down?"

"Can you dig into Immigration files to see if incoming passengers to Nova Scotia were recorded?"

"I can try. I'm not sure if those records were kept and if so whether they are available today."

"Guess where I am off to today."

"New Germany?"

"Brilliant deduction! I'll nose around to see if there are any very old people who have lived there all their lives."

"They might remember a teenager staying with Herman Hempel."

"That's what I'm hoping. I'll see you later this afternoon."

~

Jeremy Akerman

It could not have gone better. I took the Harvest Highway to North Alton, Route 12 to South Alton, the River Road through Brigadoon to Lake George, the Aylesford Road to Franey's Corner then the Barr's Corner Road to New Germany. It took me less than an hour.

New Germany is a remarkably pleasant community, with smart houses along a main road and some quite lovely churches. I went to Fresh Mart to make inquiries, but the young man behind the counter said the oldest person he knew was his grandfather, who was 75.

I wandered over to the Lutheran church, set behind a grove of rather nice trees, When I had looked around the churchyard and came back out onto the road, I walked along, enjoying this quiet spot and the warmth of the sun.

Then I noticed a very tasteful, discreet sign set in a flower bed, announcing that this was Sweeny's funeral home. A man was mowing the home's vast lawn and I stopped to talk to him.

His name was Eric Eisner and he mopped his brow with a large red handkerchief as we chatted. He reckoned that there were two residents who qualified, but that the oldest, now a hundred, was—as he put it—"out of it". The second oldest was a George Zwicker, who was 98, but "quite sharp". He told me Mr. Zwicker lived with his son in a large house about a kilometre away.

I found the house without any trouble and, as I approached I wondered if the son would present any difficulties to my speaking with his father, who, I thought, was likely bedridden in a back room.

As I got closer, a hearty voice hailed me from the veranda.

"Who you lookin' for, boy?"

"I'd like to see George Zwicker, if that's possible."

"Look no further," the man said, beckoning from a cane chair. "Come sit yourself down."

Needing no second bidding, I planted myself in a rather rickety chair next to him, delighted to find that this vigorous, healthy-looking individual was the man I was seeking.

"Now then," he said, brushing his moustache with the back of his hand, "what can I do for you?"

"Mr. Zwicker, have you lived here all your life."

"That I have. Man and boy."

"How old would you have been in the early 1930s?"

"Depends on when in the early thirties. I kep' getting older even then." He laughed heartily.

"Say in 1932."

"Well I'm 98 now so I'd ha' been six or thereabout."

"Do you remember a Herman Hempel?"

"God a'mighty. I hant heard that name in a good many years. Why you askin' 'bout him?"

"So, you do remember him?"

"Sure. Right owly he was. Never kind to little kids. Bullied the likes of I. Kep' himself to himself."

"Do you recall when he arrived in New Germany, and when he left?"

"Well, he was here before I was." He laughed. "And he would've moved on when I was 'bout ten, I guess."

"Did he ever have any visitors?"

"Visitors? I imagine people were dropping by his place from time to time."

"No, I meant relatives who came to stay with him."

"Oh, you must be talkin' 'bout Gene."

"Gene?"

"Yes, his nephew or something. Herman called him Eugen, but the folks around here called him Gene. Specially the women."

"A charmer, was he?"

"I should say so. He was only 'bout fifteen, I guess, but they was all over him like flies on a pot of jam."

"Did he stay long?"

"How do you mean?"

"Did he visit regularly?"

"My dear man, he lived here, didn't he?"

"I see." I sat back in the chair which creaked loudly. "So, he would have been here for four or five years?"

"Somethin' like that. Maybe not as many as five."

"Did you like him?"

"Well, he was a lot older than me, so he dint bother with small fry, but since you ask, no I dint."

"Sly, was he?"

"Sly. That's right. And not nice to animals."

"How so?"

"Couple of times I saw him tormenting some poor creature, or beating it with a stick. He seemed to enjoy it. I got no time for folk what is cruel to animals!"

"Mr. Zwicker, thank you very much indeed." I rose and stepped off the veranda onto the lawn. "You've been very helpful. Very helpful indeed."

15

The smell of bacon sizzling brought a tousled-headed Rosalie down to the kitchen the following morning. She sauntered over to me and peered over my shoulder.

"Ughh!" she said, looking into the second pan.

For some time I had been trying to obtain something close to the black pudding one finds in Britain, but had been unsuccessful. All imitations I could find in Nova Scotia were lighter, softer, and without the inclusions of pork fat and oatmeal which make the English variety so appetizing. Today I was trying another local product with which I hoped I would have more success.

"This one might be better," I said. "More to your taste."

"It doesn't matter how many different kinds, or how often you put it in front of me I won't eat the stuff."

"That's prejudice."

"I don't care."

"What you like for your breakfast, then?"

"I'll take that bacon and some scrambled eggs."

"Yes, Your Majesty. Will there be anything else?"

"Sourdough toast and some Saint Helena coffee."

"Okay, I think we might have some left," I said, going to the cupboard to find this exquisite product, made from Green Tipped Bourbon Arabica beans grown on an island in the South Atlantic.

"Do you think Napoleon drank it when he was exiled there?" she asked.

"Maybe that's what killed him," I said. "Are you sure you want to take the chance?"

"I think I'll risk it."

When we had finished eating our breakfasts, we took our coffee out onto the deck. It was still a little cool, but it was very bracing, and we imagined we could smell the salt from the sea only three kilometres away.

"So, since John Bland, or Gene, or Eugen—let's call him Eugen from now on—didn't appear in the 1931 census with Hermann Hempel, we must conclude that he didn't arrive in New Germany until after June that year."

"Why June?" I asked.

"Because that was the month in which the census was conducted."

"Okay. Right."

"And you said Mr. Zwicker told you that Eugen was not there for as long as five years?"

"Yes, that's right."

"So, if he arrived in or around late 1931 or early 1932, he would have been gone by 1936 at the latest?"

"That makes sense. Yes."

"Now, while you were gallivanting about in New Germany yesterday—"

"I was not gallivanting, I'll have you know. I was doing serious research."

"Like I say, while you were cavorting with nonagenarians, I did some digging into ships arriving in Halifax from Germany."

"You have been a busy bee. What did you find out?"

"Assuming he did land in Halifax—and we don't know that for sure; he could have landed in Montreal and got the train from there—assuming he did land in Halifax, there were remarkably few German vessels which arrived in the period from mid-June

1931 to 1933."

"How many?"

"Total of four."

"Where did they sail from?"

"Each of them sailed from Hamburg."

"And?"

"I couldn't find any ship's lists which gave the ages of passengers, and before you ask, yes, there were more than a dozen single men on board those ships."

"And because we don't know what his surname was, you couldn't get any further?"

"That's right. You didn't ask Mr. Zwicker what surname he went by, did you?"

"Damn! I didn't think of it. I'll see if I can get him on the phone today."

"What else are you planning to do today?"

"I have to pick up the deeds to the book shop from Walter Bryden's law firm, then take them to Gerald."

"That was a nice gesture on your part, Marc. To give Gerald the shop outright."

"Well, I couldn't attend to it—it would drive me nuts—and it doesn't make much of a profit, so there wasn't much point in maintaining a share in the business."

"It's strange how life creates unexpected opportunities. If your brother hadn't died, the shop would not have come to you, and you wouldn't have been able to give it to Gerald."

I said nothing, knowing that my older brother, Lawrence, was not dead at all. A secret I had to keep forever, even from Rosalie, was that Larry was an international criminal who had his death certificate forged by experts in Europe, and sent to Walter Bryden to submit to the court. The court had then ruled that the eldest son was dead, and that as a consequence my father's estate, including the book shop, should devolve on me.

Although I did not think my secrets were in the same league as John Bland's, I reflected that, in all likelihood, most people had their own.

I asked Rosalie to try to find a telephone number for George Zwicker, indicating to her that it would not be in his name, but that I did not know his son's first name. I gave her the address I had visited yesterday and she went to work on the computer.

"Good Lord!" she exclaimed after a few minutes. "Do you know how many Zwickers there are in the New Germany area?"

"No. How many?"

"Dozens of them! But this one corresponds with the address you gave me. Robert Zwicker."

"That'll be it. I'll call now."

I dialed the number and waited for what seemed an inordinate amount of time.

"Hello." It was a young voice.

"Good morning, I am sorry to disturb you. May I speak to Mr. Zwicker please?"

"This is him speaking."

"No, I wanted to speak with Mr. George Zwicker. I was talking to him only yesterday."

"Then you were probably the last person to see him alive. My father died yesterday, around 3 pm."

16

As it turned out, one thing and another prevented me from going to see Gerald the previous day, so I called Walter Bryden at home and asked him if he would mind meeting me at his office this morning, and let me have me the deeds to the shop.

"Can't it wait until Monday?" he asked.

I suspected he was itching to get on to the golf course. "It'll only take two minutes, Walter. I've promised Gerald I would deal with it, and I'd rather not put it off again."

"Alright. I'll see you there in ten minutes."

I had guessed right. Walter was standing outside his office in his golfing clothes, with his spiked shoes hanging over his shoulder and his glove sticking out of his breast pocket. His car was parked nearby and I could see his clubs on the passenger seat.

"Come on," he said brusquely. "I don't have all day."

"What is your tee time?"

"In five minutes," he growled.

He opened the door and led me up the stairs. "I still think you're making a mistake. You could get two million for that old store any day. It's in a prime location."

"I don't need the money, Walter."

"Yes, but giving the shop to a stranger?"

"Gerald isn't a stranger. He was my father's right hand man."

"Enough said!" Walter barked and let himself into the office.

He handed me the papers, indicating the places where I should

Jeremy Akerman

sign. I took them from him and put them in my attaché case.

"How is my investment in the winery, Walter?" This was a reference to the property in the Gaspereau Valley of my former friend, John Dempster, in which I had bought a 25% share.

"Still struggling a bit as a result of last year's frost kill, but the business now seems to be on a relatively sound footing. Why don't you go up and check it out for yourself?"

"Ah no. I no longer have contact with John, although I occasionally see Jean Pierre, the winemaker, in town."

"Well, it's none of my business. I guess you know what you are doing."

"Yes, I do. Many thanks for doing this, Walter."

I then walked across the street to see Gerald at the shop.

He was wildly excited that his dream was finally, officially, settled. "I'll never know how to thank you, Marc."

"Someday, some way, there may be a favour I need from you."

"Any time. You just say the word. I must go put these documents in the safe."

"Before you do that, Gerald, do you have any books about German spies in the Valley during World War II?'

"What valley?"

"Our valley. The Annapolis Valley."

"Good heavens, no! Were there any German spies here?"

"Maybe. Keep an eye open for me. If anything like that comes your way, please let me know."

My duty to Gerald done, I drove out to a little farm near Upper Falmouth where I had been told one could buy pheasants for the table. There are few morsels as delicious as a carefully roasted pheasant with a nice, brown, crispy skin, served with creamed cabbage and roast Yukon Gold potatoes, or braised with wild mushrooms in white wine.

I found the place with some difficulty, it being hidden by trees at the end of a long, winding lane. A man came out from behind the barn armed with a 12 bore shotgun. Apparently, he had never seen a Bugatti before and found its appearance suspicious.

After being assured that I was not "from the government", he led me into a small paddock and pointed to a flock of birds, all strutting about, pecking in the grass for seeds and grubs. There were beautiful ring-necked pheasants, ducks, geese, gray partridges whose wings had been clipped, and a host of little quail under a protective net covering.

"Tell me what you want and I'll catch 'em and kill 'em for you," said the farmer, who told me his name was Harold Aikens.

"Will you also draw and pluck them for me?" I asked.

"Sure, if'n you're squeamish. But it'll take a bit of time and I'll have to charge you for the labour."

"That's okay. I'll take a brace each of pheasants, partridges, ducks; one goose, and half a dozen quail," I said, knowing I had ample space for them in my Ikon - 81" freezer in the basement.

"That'll be about two hours unless I gets the Mrs. to give me a hand."

"That would be wonderful."

"Alright, I'll ask her. Meantime why don't you take a stroll round the farm? If you take that there path, it'll take you to the river."

I spent several very pleasant hours wandering along the West Branch of the Avon River, spending the time observing a variety of wildlife, including mallards, black ducks, a kestrel, a kingfisher and an assortment of sparrows, warblers and fly catchers.

By the time I got back to the farm, Harold had the birds drawn, plucked, trussed, and displayed on a trestle. His wife, a large, bouncy woman wearing a permanent smile, stood behind it.

Harold asked $250 for the lot, which, under the circumstances, I thought was very reasonable.

I asked him to put them into two sacks, which I would distribute between the trunk and the passenger seat. Considerately, he first wrapped them in plastic bags to prevent leakage, put them in the sacks and then humped them into the car.

With a hearty wave they bade me goodbye and I roared off, more than satisfied with my morning's work.

~

That evening, before we went to pick up Leslie Alsop, Rosalie and I had an early dinner of just one of the partridges, roasted with bacon and pears and served with peas and sautéed potatoes. Since she had agreed to drive, I had a large glass of Domaine de Romanee Conti La Tache 2005, which was utterly superb. The rest I preserved, using a rubber cap and an air pump; wine of this calibre and price should not be wasted!

We found Leslie waiting outside the University main entrance. He was carrying his laden backpack, but looked somewhat different from the last time we had seen him. As he climbed into the back of the BMW, I noticed that he had removed his cheek rings, trimmed his beard and shortened his ponytail, and I wondered if the sobering subject matter of his research had caused this transformation.

"Good evening, Leslie," I said.

"Hey. What's shaking?"

"That's what I should be asking you. Have you found anything interesting?"

"Have I ever!" Leslie said. "Although there's so much material, I didn't have time to read very much of it in detail."

"But you have a general idea?"

"I think so. Do you want me to go into it now or wait until we get to Mr. Bland's house?"

"We'd better wait. We'll be there in a few minutes."

As we pulled into Ray's driveway, there was a gleaming, latest-model Alpina B8 Gran Coupe parked by the garage. Ray came out to meet us and we exchanged greetings.

"How much for the car, Ray?"

"Why? Are you interested in trading yours in?"

"I might be. That's a real beauty."

"She certainly is. I could let you have it for $237,846."

"Wow!" Leslie exclaimed.

"How much for my BMW if I traded it in?" I asked.

"We'd have to work it out. Let me know if you're serious."

"Okay. I'll think about it."

"Let's go in. Rachel has coffee and desserts, if you are still hungry. Or something stronger, if you want."

"Can I have both?" Leslie asked, like a kid in a candy store.

"Sure," Ray said, laughing.

When we were settled around a big table in the dining room and each had taken what drinks and pastries they wanted, Ray pushed some papers across the table to Leslie.

"Enough chit chat and small talk. We all know why we're here. First of all, Leslie, I want you to sign this confidentiality agreement."

"Okay, boss," Leslie said, signing in the appropriate places.

"That seems to be in order," said Ray, after examining the document. "So, Leslie, tell us what we've got."

"You've got a whole whack of stuff. Mountains of it. As I told Mr. LeBlanc, I could only read a fraction of it."

"Give the Coles Notes version."

"Okay. First we've got a series of code books, all without the keys, so they won't be of any use to us.

"Then we have notebooks, four of them, closely written in an abbreviated German. They are very difficult to understand.

"Then we have a diary—quite long—which would seem to cover

many years.

"Then we have three photographs."

"Photos of people?" Rachel asked.

"No. No people. One is of what seems certain is a campus of a university."

"Can you identify which one?"

"Unfortunately, I can't. As far as I can see, it could be one of a number of European universities."

"Okay. What were the others?" Ray asked.

"Two castles."

"Can you identify these?"

"Yes, I can identify one of them. It's definitely Regensburg castle."

"Where's Regensburg?" Rosalie inquired.

"In Germany," replied Leslie. "Regensburg is in eastern Bavaria, in southern Germany where the Danube, Naab and Reben_rivers meet. It's the capital of the Upper Palatinate_sub-region of the state."

He passed the photograph and we all took a look at it. The castle, on several levels of a rocky outcrop, had red tiled roofs and a tower.

He passed us the other photograph. This castle looked smaller and older, with two towers, one larger than the other, and was dramatically situated on a cliff overlooking a lake or river.

"Where's this?" I asked.

"No idea," said Leslie, "I've searched the internet for German castles and I came up with zilch. I'll keep looking, but I'm not hopeful."

"Okay. What next?" Ray prompted.

"Ah. This is very interesting. There was a large envelope containing various badges, flashes and epaulettes."

"What do they tell us?" Rachel asked.

"These are collar flashes."

He passed us two black felt rectangles, one with a silver square in each corner, and the other with two parallel zigzags. Then he pushed across a rectangular, black cloth bearing a green bar surmounted by two parallel sets of two acorns, each flanked by oak leaves.

"Then there's these two epaulettes."

These were clearly from the shoulders of a uniform and were made of interwoven silver thread on black.

"What does this all mean?" asked Rosalie.

"It means," said Leslie, "that whoever owned these was a *sturmbannfuhrer* in the *Schutzstaffel*."

"A what in the what?" asked Ray impatiently.

"I know," said Rachel with a shudder. "It means he was a major in the Waffen SS."

"Jesus!" Ray cursed.

"That's right," said Leslie. "But there's one more flash. This would have been worn on the sleeve between the shoulder and elbow."

He showed us a rather nondescript, diamond-shaped piece of cloth which bore the letters SD.

"What does this mean?"

"The SD stands for the *Sicherheitsdienst*. It was the emblem of the *Sicherheitsdients des Reichfuhrers Shutzstaffel*. They were the Foreign Security Service."

"What the hell did they do?"

"They were responsible for intelligence activities outside the Reich. Sometimes called *Abteilung* VI, or Department Six. You may be interested to learn that, until his death in June of 1942, the Department was commanded by Reinhard Heydrich."

"That bastard!" Rachel almost spat.

"Indeed. But if we are talking about a period from late 1942 onward, Heydrich was gone and the Department had long been subsumed by the *Reichssicherheotshauptamt*, or the National Security service, headed by the charming Heinrich Himmler. The gentleman actually running the department was Walter Schellenberg."

"It's a wonder the Nazis got as far as they did with all the red tape and bureaucracy they created," Rosalie said.

"Yes, it's incredible. Schellenburg's outfit would have worked closely and collaborated with the *Abweher*, led by Admiral Canaris."

"He was a cunning old fox, by all accounts," I said.

"Yes, he more or less put together and shaped Germany's intelligence and counterintelligence machinery."

"I'm confused," Ray confessed. "Does this mean that the guy who had the envelope full of these flashes and badges was a Major in the SS who somehow transferred to this Sicherheits thing?"

"Unless he stole or bought the insignia, yes."

"And where does this Canary guy come into it?"

"Canaris," Leslie corrected. "In 1942, Canaris launched Operation Pastorius, which was to spy on or sabotage targets in North America. Largely, it was a failure, because two of the men he sent to the United States snitched on their buddies and the FBI nabbed them. All but two of them were executed by the electric chair in Washington."

"What about Canada?"

"The documentation is not as clear as it is for the United States. But from what I can gather, Canaris sent several agents to Canada. Only one of them is accounted for."

"One?"

"Yes, he was Alfred Langbein, who was landed from a U-boat somewhere in the Maritimes."

"What happened to him?"

"He was entirely the wrong sort of guy for the Germans to send as a spy because, the minute he landed, he dumped his radio and went to live on the Ottawa River, where he used the money the Abweher had given him to set up house. When the money had gone, he turned himself into the Mounties."

"What a story!" I said. "But you said there were others unaccounted for."

"Yes. I can't discover how many there were, but I get the impression that there were three or four."

"That's good work, Leslie," said Ray. "I'm very grateful to you, even if what you tell me doesn't sit very well. After all, it's not every day you find out your Grandpa was a SS Major."

"I'm afraid there's more," said Leslie quietly.

"More? What do you mean?"

"I debated with myself whether to tell you about this at this stage in the work, but I think you ought to know, because you might not want me to continue."

"Why would I do that?"

"It's not very pleasant."

"You think it has been pleasant so far?"

"No, I guess not."

"Come on then. Out with it!"

"There are two more pieces of information that my research has uncovered. There will likely be many more, as I have only scratched the surface so far."

"What are they?"

"One, from the German government, is a certificate attesting that the bearer is a graduate of a recognized German medical school. Unfortunately, it doesn't say which one. And there is no name given."

"What's the other?"

Leslie took a deep breath and hesitated for a few seconds. He frowned, then spoke almost in a whisper as if he were embarrassed. "In one of the early diaries I saw an entry which said : *Das bedeutet, dass ich die Forschung, die ich im Camp durchgeführt habe, fortsetzen kann.*"

"What does that mean?"

"That means 'I can continue the research I did at the camp'."

"Camp. What camp?" Ray demanded.

There was an unholy silence for several minutes which was broken by Rachel's cry.

"*Oy, meyn gott*! A concentration camp. He was one of those camp doctors who experimented on inmates!"

"You mean like Mengele?" Rosalie was aghast.

"Yes," said Leslie. "I'm pretty sure that's what it means."

"Dear God," Ray said. "What have I done, opening this up? When I started, I knew there was something not right about my grandfather, but I never dreamed it would be this."

"Do you want me to quit?" Leslie asked.

"No. I may as well know the whole truth."

"You realize that it could get worse?"

"I guess so. But we've begun so we may as well finish. Carry on, Leslie...wherever it leads."

17

After I got up the next morning, I switched on the radio to get the news while I was shaving, and almost immediately I heard an item to the effect that Israel had killed eleven Palestinians and the UN Secretary General Antonio Gutierres and US President Biden had condemned Israel's 'disproportionate violence'.

I decided to discuss this with Rachel, because it put Israel in a poor light, and I wondered how she would explain it. In any event, I wanted to talk to her about the so-called 'Pre 1967 Green Line', about which I had been recently reading.

The Green Line was the demarcation set out in the 1949 Armistice Agreements between the armies of Israel and those of its neighbours, Egypt, Jordan, Lebanon and Syria, after the 1948 Arab–Israeli War, in which seven Arab nations attacked Israel. It was the de facto border of Israel from 1949 until the Six-Day War in 1967, when Israel took back Judea and Samaria from Jordan, which had occupied them in 1948. The Green Line was recognized internationally as Israel's borders and was the territorial limit to which many demanded that Israel should withdraw.

As Rosalie was making sounds of rising, I cast my mind back over what we had learned from Leslie the previous evening, and how we might be able to expand upon it.

Then, I remembered that the famous Holocaust survivor and Nazi hunter, Simon Wiesenthal, had set up the Documentation Centre of the Association of Jewish Victims of the Nazi Regime in

Vienna in 1961 and had continued to try to locate missing Nazi war criminals until his death in 2005. If his organization had not died with him, I thought we might be able to submit our information to them and ask them if they could identify John Bland, or Eugen, from that.

I mentioned this to Rosalie over our breakfast of omelettes loaded with freshly grated Gruyere cheese and quickly-sautéed baby tomatoes. She said she would look into it as soon as she had finished eating, then she gave me an odd look.

"What's up with you today?"

"How do you mean?"

"Clearly, something is agitating you. What is it?"

"Nothing."

"Obviously it's not nothing. What's happened?"

I explained about the news item on the Middle East and said I couldn't imagine how Rachel could justify what had occurred.

"Maybe she won't justify it. Maybe it's just one of those occasional unfortunate mistakes."

"I don't think so. It is very similar to other reports I have heard on CBC."

"Well, don't sit here brooding. It's Sunday, so she'll be home. Go and see her while I'm checking out the Wiesenthal organization."

"Alright. I will."

~

There was very little traffic and, using the Harvest Highway, I got to Ray and Rachel's place in seven minutes flat, and pulled up behind the new BMW Alpina. They were surprised to see me, but welcomed me in and brewed more coffee.

"What is it, Marc? Developments in the case?"

"No, not yet, but Rosalie is contacting Nazi-hunting organizations today to see if they can identify your granddad."

"That will be interesting. You'll let me know what she discovers?"

"Of course." I took a sip of coffee. "Actually, I came to see Rachel. I wanted to discuss something I heard on the news this morning."

"I can guess what it is," said Rachel grimly, "I was on the phone to my cousins in Israel at eight this morning. It was two in the afternoon there. One of them, Avi, is a commander in the IDF."

"What's the IDF?"

"The Israeli Defence Forces. Now, calm down, Marc, and tell me exactly what you heard."

I repeated the newscast word for word, having scribbled down a few notes so I would get it right. "Fighting has broken out again in the middle-east. Eleven Palestinians have been killed by the Israeli Air Force and two Israelis are dead. UN Secretary General Antonio Gutierres and President Biden have condemned Israel's disproportionate violence and called for both sides to exercise restraint."

"Okay. Let's start at the beginning," said Rachel. "What happened was that at shortly after 11 at night, Israeli time, eighteen rockets were launched by Hamas from Gaza at Ashkelon and Sderot. These are cities in the southwest of Israel. Ashkelon has a population of 130,000, Sderot about 30,000. These are both residential areas, where there are no military facilities, large army bases, or military infrastructure. Hamas targets civilians."

"But—"

"Please let me finish, Marc."

"Sorry. Go on."

"Fortunately, all but one of these rockets were destroyed in the air by Israel's 'Iron Dome' defence system. The one which wasn't caught hit Shikmim, a suburb of Ashkelon, killing two people. In the meantime, the IDF had identified the location from which the rockets were launched and, after 'roof knocking' the area, the Air

Force was dispatched to bomb the target."

"Roof knocking? What's that?"

"Before every strike, the IAF targets a building with a loud but non-lethal bomb that warns civilians that they are in the vicinity of a weapons cache or other target. This method is used to allow all residents to leave the area before the IDF targets the site with live ammunition."

"Good grief! They do that every time?"

"Every time."

"Who else does that to their enemy?"

"The IDF is the only military force I know that does."

"Jesus! I had no idea."

"Anyway, it appears Hamas would not let a number of civilians heed the warning, so three of them were caught in the raid. The others killed were Hamas members. Terrorists."

"I don't know what to say. But you can see why the UN says the response was 'disproportionate' when only two Israelis were killed as opposed to 11 Palestinians."

"Look, Marc, Israel spends millions and millions on the Iron Dome and millions more on underground shelters which are mandated by law. People can go to these during a rocket attack."

"Yes, but surely Gaza has similar shelters."

"Only for the Hamas leadership. The billions of dollars it gets from around the world goes to offensive weapons and into the pockets of the terrorist bosses."

"What?"

"The titular leader of Hamas, Ismail Haniyeh, who spends his time in Turkey and Qatar, has personal wealth estimated at $6 million. Khaled Mashaal, the current leader in Gaza, is worth $2.3 billion, and his co-leader, Mousa Abu Marzouq, is worth well over a billion. And, according to his financial advisor, Mahmoud Abbas is personally worth $100 million U.S. In case you didn't know it, Abbas is the man who bankrolled the Munich Massacre at the 1972 Olympics."

"But aren't the Gazans poor?"

"Most of them are. But not the leaders. The point is that Hamas has ample money to provide shelters for its people but doesn't, so they get killed in greater numbers than Israelis because they do have shelters. When people say the casualties are 'disproportionate', what they are really saying is that they want more dead Jews to make the numbers even."

Since I could not refute this inference, I said nothing, so drank some more coffee.

"Was there anything else, Marc?" I could tell that Rachel was annoyed at my persistence, but I pressed on.

"I just wanted to ask about the pre 1967 'Green Line', and why Israel refuses to pull back to it."

"Apart from the fact that the land it would have to give up has belonged to the Jews for 3,000 years"—Rachel was now furious—"the distance from the 'Green Line' to the sea is only 14 kilometres."

"So?"

"So? So? Many Arab terror attacks have originated in Judea and Samaria, which are in close proximity to Israeli population centres. This narrow part of central Israel, stretching along the coastline between Hadera and Gedera, includes the city of Tel Aviv, Ben Gurion Airport and the heart of Israel's economic life. Millions of Israelis live and work there.

"Actually, nearly all of Israel's major towns, as well as most of the strategic locations in the country, are within firing range of the Green Line. The airport is only about 6 km away.

"You saw today that rockets from Gaza could hit Ashkelon, which is 21 kilometres away. It stands to reason that even short-range rockets or mortar shells could paralyze Israel, should she revert to the pre-1967 border."

"I see," I said slowly. "There would be no guarantee—no likelihood—that an Arab state with a border that close would not be hostile."

"Smart boy!" Rachel said irritably. "And the record indicates that the chances of such a state being friendly would be 1,000 to one against. To allow such a thing would be utter madness."

"But we don't know half of this, here in the west. At best, our media gives us half-truths. I can't understand why that would be."

"You already know my answer to that. It is also the answer to why, alone among the peoples of the earth, Jews are required to explain and justify everything they think, say and do, and everything they have thought, said and done throughout history. Now, if you'll excuse me, I have a lot to do."

"I'm sorry Rachel if I've been an ass."

"That's okay, Marc. You're in good company."

When I got back home to Grand Pre, Rosalie greeted me with the news that she had made contact with the Documentation Centre of the Association of Jewish Victims of the Nazi Regime, she said, was an integral, but independent, part of the Vienna Wiesenthal Institute for Holocaust studies.

She told me she had given them the details of John Bland and expected a response within a few hours. Vienna was five hours ahead of Nova Scotia, but they informed her that everyone there worked late. It was a matter of seeing if their computer could match Bland's information with any Nazi who had been convicted at the Nuremberg trials *in absentia*, or indeed any Nazi who was suspected of war crimes, but, for one reason or another, had not been put on trial.

The reply came through at what would have been after eleven o'clock Vienna time.

Thank you for your request to the Dokumentationszentrum des Bundes Jüdischer Verfolgter des Naziregimes. With respect to your inquiry re. John Bland, two persons in our records meet the following criteria:

Born in or near Bavaria between 1910 and 1920.

Possession of Medical Degree from a recognized German University.

Connections with Regensburg.

Sturmbannfuhrer in the Schutzstaffel.

Subsequent membership in Sicherheitsdients des Reichfuhrers Shutzstaffel.

Associated with one or more Konzentrationslagers (concentration camps) in a medical capacity.

Known visits to Canada prior to 1930.

(A) Walter E. Klemper. Born Blaibach 1914. Graduated in medicine Heidelberg University 1933. Joined SS 1939. Assigned to Ravensbruck 1941. Assistant to Dr. Karl Franz Gebhardt. Convicted to hang in absentia, Nuremberg 1947. Last report 1942. Whereabouts unknown.

(B) Eugen M. Dieter. Born Regensburg 1913. Graduated in medicine Regensburg University 1932. Joined SS 1938. Assigned to Dachau 1940. Assistant to Dr. Sigmund Rascher. Convicted to hang in absentia Nuremberg 1947. Last report 1942. Whereabouts unknown.

"Well," said Rosalie. "What do you think of that?"

"It's a step closer, but at first glance it could be either of these guys."

"Or neither of them. These are all they have on record. There could be others who fell through the cracks."

"Which one do you fancy for John Bland?"

"I think it has to be Eugen Dieter. He has more points of contact —if I can use that expression."

"I agree. Discrepancies of a year here and there can be overlooked because we don't know for certain how old Bland was when he died."

"Dachau! That was the worst camp of all next to Auschwitz, If I recall correctly. This guy sure isn't becoming any more likeable as time goes on!"

"We'd better give Ray a call and bring him up to date."

"And Leslie. He needs to be kept in the loop too."

18

We had all agreed to meet again on Monday at Ray and Rachel's place to review what Rosalie had learned from Vienna and what information Leslie had been able to find to flesh out our knowledge of Major Eugen Dieter of the Waffen SS.

As before, Rosalie and I picked up Leslie in Wolfville in our BMW. But this time, I was positively amazed by the transformation in his appearance: He had trimmed his beard very closely and had completely cut off the ponytail, and had made a not wholly successful effort to hide the neck tattoo.

When we were welcomed at the front door, Leslie said he could not stay more than an hour as he had to attend his mother's birthday party in town. Ray said he would take Leslie back so Rosalie and I could stay longer and socialize.

As we were filing into the dining room to take out places around the shiny, large, oval table, I noticed that Rachel was looking at me oddly. I feared it meant that I offended her on my visit yesterday, so I hung back and followed her into the kitchen.

"Rachel, I hope I didn't upset you yesterday."

"Upset me? Of course you didn't upset me. But, Marc, something else has upset me and I want to talk to you about it."

"What is it, Rachel? Has something happened?"

"I haven't told Ray. He would get too worked up. But I need to tell someone."

"Sure. When?"

"When Ray runs Leslie back into Wolfville, I'll offer to show you the lower garden and the pond. Rosalie has already seen it, so it might work."

"Alright. We'd better go in now, or they might think we're having an affair."

Rachel laughed uproariously and went ahead of me into the dining room.

"Okay," said Ray. "I have distributed glasses and I have nice bottle of Chardonnay from the Blomidon winery. Since Leslie has to go to his mom's birthday party, I propose we start right away by hearing everything he has put together."

"Right," said Leslie. "Eugen Dieter was born near Regensburg in Bavaria in a small place called Bach an der Donau, on the Danube, in July of 1913—roughly a year before the start of World War One.

"He attended local schools and took pre-med and medical courses at Regensburg University, graduating in May of 1938. It was then he appears to have been recruited into the SS, largely on account of his medical qualifications. Again, due to his education he joined as an *Untersturmfuhrer*, or Second Junior Assault Officer, the equivalent of a Second Lieutenant in the Wehrmacht, or army.

"By 1938 he had risen to being a *Obersturmfuhrer* or First Lieutenant, in 1939 to *Hauptsurmfuhrer* or Captain, and in 1940 to *Sturmbannfuhrer* or Major.

"In mid-1940—I don't have the exact date—he was assigned to the Dachau concentration camp, which was in Upper Bavaria, not far from his home. There he was a member of a team which assisted Dr. Sigmund Rascher.

"Rascher was a particularly unsavoury character, who specialized in deadly experiments on humans at high altitudes, studying the freezing and blood coagulation which happened under those conditions. It was thought his experiments would help the Luftwaffe be able to fly their planes higher. Apparently, he was a favourite of *Reichsführer-SS* Heinrich Himmler. Rascher's wife, Karoline 'Nini' Diehl, had direct connections with Himmler over a long period.

"The Raschers pretended to have discovered an unnatural fertility, and boasted that Karoline had given birth to three children after the age of 48, but it was discovered that they had hired or kidnapped the babies. He was arrested in April, 1944, accused of financial irregularities and the murder of one his former lab assistants, and was executed.

"Somewhere along the way—I cannot be accurate on the date—Dieter volunteered for the *Sicherheitsdienst*, Department Six, and went to work for foreign intelligence. How he got involved with Canaris' Operation Pastorius is unclear, and for security reasons records of his overseas activities would have been few and far between. In any event, they have not survived. But this all fits with his coming on the U-boat *Feinste* in 1942.

"I found an early photograph of him. The quality is not good, but I am guessing he would have been about 25 at the time. As you can see, it is a posed shot of him pretending to shoot some game birds."

Leslie pushed the photo across the table and we passed it around. In it, a young blond man had a shotgun to his shoulder. It looked as if it might have been taken near woodlands.

"Ray, does it look like your grandfather?" I asked.

"God knows. He was near 80 when I last saw him and I was seven, so I can't remember one way or the other. But I do remember my mother saying he was left-handed and this guy is holding the gun to this right shoulder. So that fits."

"Anything else, Leslie?" Rachel asked.

"I'd like to leave comment on the notebooks until I understand them better. There are some abbreviations which I haven't yet grasped and some of the terms are technical."

"How about the diaries?" Rosalie asked.

"I've left this subject 'til last because it makes very disturbing reading. I must warn you that the inferences to be drawn from some of the entries are shocking."

"I don't suppose anyone wants to leave the room or anything like that, so you may as well go ahead," Ray said.

"I can't go into every entry, obviously, but for now I have picked a few which seem relevant."

"That makes sense. There must be hours of reading in them."

"There is, yes."

"Well, give us your chosen snippets."

"Okay. Here goes. I'll translate as I go along."

> 5. Mai 1945
>
> Habe heute eine junge Frau gesehen. Unattraktiv. Sehr leicht und schlicht.
>
> Saw a young woman today. Unattractive. Very slight and plain.
>
> Ich hätte es nicht weiter beachtet, aber ich habe gehört, dass sie ZWEI Geschwister mit Progerie hat. Davon bin ich aufgrund meiner Arbeit im Lager begeistert.
>
> Would have taken no further notice but I heard she had TWO siblings with progeria. Am excited by this because of my work in the camp.

"Then a few pages later, we get this:"

> 8. Mai 1945
> Habe das Mädchen wieder gesehen. Mit den beiden Schwestern mit Progeria. Erbärmliche Kleinigkeiten. Sie stammen aus einer

Unspeakable Evil

Familie mit fünf Kindern. Das Gen muss da sein.

Saw the girl again. With the two sisters with Progeria. Pathetic little things. They are from a family of five children. The gene must be there.

Ich werde mich ihr gegenüber angenehm machen, auch wenn es eine Anstrengung sein könnte.

Will make myself pleasant to her even though it might be an effort.

Ich kann mir nicht vorstellen, dass irgendjemand anders an ihr interessiert wäre, also dürfte es für mich kein Problem sein, ihr Vertrauen zu gewinnen.

Don't imagine anyone else would be interested in her so I should have no problem worming my way into her confidence.

"And:"

20. Mai 1945

Es ist erledigt. Wir wollen in zwei Monaten heiraten. Ich habe es mit dem Pfarrer vereinbart. Er zeigte sich überrascht über meine Wahl, aber er weiß nicht, welche Belohnungen ich von der Ehe erwarte. Ich habe vor, sofort mit der Zucht zu beginnen. Und dann kann ich meine Arbeit fortsetzen.

It is settled. We are to be married in two months. I have arranged it with the pastor. He showed surprise at my choice, but he does not know what rewards I expect from the marriage. I intend to start breeding immediately. And then I can continue my work.

"My God!" Rachel's cry was full of anguish.
"What does this mean?" Asked Rosalie.
"I don't think there is any other way to interpret this," said Leslie. "I think this man deliberately married a woman he didn't care for—didn't even like—in the hope that at least one of her offspring would have a horrible degenerative disease."
"But why?"
"So he could experiment on the children, Rosalie," I said.
"Christ! I can't believe it!"
"I think we had better leave it there for now," Ray said. "It's a lot to take in and we're all upset. Disgusted would be a better word."
"I have to go now, anyway," Leslie said. "Ray, will you drive me to town?"
"Sure. It'll help to calm me down."
They got up and went out into the forecourt. As Ray started the car, Rachel gave me a slight nod. Then she said, "Rosalie, can I get you a whisky? You look very pale."
"Yes please. I think I need one."
Rachel made the drink and passed it to Rosalie.
"Marc, you haven't seen our pond, have you? We have some lovely lilies growing in it."
"No, I haven't, but I'd like to."
"Rosalie has already seen it so, while she's having her Scotch, why don't we go down the garden?"
"Yes, you go ahead. I'm a little unsteady so I'll just sit here and drink," Rosalie said.
"We won't be long, darling."

~

When we were out of sight of the dining room window, Rachel guided me to one side of the garden and took a piece of paper out of her pocket. "Read this."

I took it and unfolded it. I was totally unprepared for what I saw. It read:

> *Mind your own business, you Jew bitch. Isn't the genocide in Gaza enough for you?*

"What the hell is this? Where did you get it?"

"I found it on my desk at the hospital this afternoon."

"Do you have any idea where it came from?"

"None. For God's sake, don't tell Ray. He'd go through the roof."

"Who could blame him? This is disgusting. What's all this about genocide in Gaza?"

"The 'Palestinians' and their supporters claim that the Jews of Israel have committed genocide against the people of Gaza. It's one of their most repeated libels."

"What do you mean? Libels?"

"Well, doesn't genocide mean a deliberate killing of large numbers of people of a particular ethnicity with the aim of exterminating them?"

"Yes, that's my understanding. But is there any truth to the allegation?"

"Marc, in 1970 there were 340,000 Arabs in Gaza. Last year there were 2,200,000. You tell me if that sounds like genocide!"

"No, I admit it doesn't. Have you received any letters like this before?"

"From time to time. Mostly it's verbal comments. It's getting worse. Did you know that in Canada last year B'nai Brith recorded over 2,800 anti-Semitic incidents, of which the Canadian govern-

Jeremy Akerman

ment recognized 608 as actual hate crimes?"

"Good God. Surely not that many?"

"Oh yes. Hate crimes against Jews is at the very top of the list. More than twice as many as against blacks and many more than against gays. And among those targeting religious communities, 62% of offences were against Jews as opposed to 16% against Muslims."

"I had no idea. Why?"

"It's been going on for centuries. When anything goes wrong, crops fail or the economy is bad, the Jews have always been a convenient scapegoat."

"You read about it occurring in Medieval times, but not in this day and age."

"I'm afraid the libels are continuing on the internet. The same old rubbish about Jews poisoning wells and stealing babies to make Matzah out of their blood."

"What's Matzah?"

"It's like crackers. Unleavened bread that's eaten during Passover."

"I confess all this is a revelation to me, Rachel. I know Jews are often accused of owning all the banks, but I've never actually researched it."

"Another libel. Of *Forbes*' famous fifty top billionaires only ten are Jews. And if you go by religion, 55% of the world's wealth is owned by Christians, 5.8% by Muslims, 3.3% by Hindus and only 1.1% by Jews."

"That surprises me. I thought it would be much higher."

"Why?"

"Er...I don't know."

"It is because even you, Marc, have a tiny spark of anti-Semitism within you."

"I guess most of us have been brought up to believe in an unsavoury connection between Jews and money."

"It's a mild form of prejudice, but prejudice nonetheless. But the more vicious forms of anti-Semitism are very much on the increase, especially in universities. The pandemic was a great vehicle for anti-Semitism because a lot of people blamed Israel and the Jews for causing the virus."

"That's crazy!"

"Crazy or not, it happened."

"What does the note mean: 'Mind your own business'?"

"I'm not sure, but it would seem to apply to our investigation of Eugen Dieter."

"Damn! Joyce Glennister and her big mouth again!"

"Joyce? Do you think she's been gossiping?"

"She always has in the past. There's no reason to think she has changed her ways."

"That is most unfortunate. I'll make a note that she is not to be trusted with anything sensitive."

"But wait a minute. When we discussed this at our dinner party we didn't know any of the history of Ray's grandfather."

"You think someone else is duplicating our research?"

"Or is getting access to Leslie's computer, more like."

"We must warn him right away."

"I'll call him tonight. He'll be at his mother's for a few hours."

"We'd better go back to the house. Ray'll be back from Wolfville any minute."

We sauntered back across the manicured lawn, which was now showing long shadows from the surrounding trees. The air was redolent with the perfume of flowers. It was a perfect early summer's evening.

"Tell me, Rachel, are these revelations about Eugen Dieter painful to you?"

"To a certain extent, yes. People like him tortured and executed millions of my people, so obviously I despise him. But at the same time, I recognize that nastiness is a human characteristic which is not inherited. I don't see anything like that in Ray."

"I'm glad to hear that. He's a great guy."

"Yes, he's very special. And I know that whatever his grandfather did, is not in any way Ray's fault."

19

I was unable to reach Leslie the night before. I guessed he had his phone switched off because of his mother's birthday party, but I left a message.

He returned my call at 6 am. "Marc? What's up?"

"You're up early."

"Yeah. Actually, I just got in. The party's still going."

"Must be some celebration."

"My Mom's forty-fifth. They were pushing the boat out."

"Look, Leslie. Something's come up. It looks as if word about our project has got out. I'm sure you haven't said anything—"

"No, I haven't. Not a breath."

"—but I wondered how secure your computer is."

"Now you mention it, not very, I guess. I leave it lying around and anyone here could have looked over my shoulder sometime and got my password."

"Where do you live?"

"In a house belonging to the University. On Highland Avenue."

"How many live there with you?"

"Most of the time there are seven or eight. I think most of them are post graduates."

"Give me a run-down on them."

"I can't name names now. Some of the guys are here. I'll draw up a list and meet you later."

"Agreed. Where and when?"

"The Naked Crêpe Bistro. At ten."

Before I went to meet Leslie, an idea struck me. It had been a long time since I had spoken with Sergeant Patrick Kennedy. He had been the lead officer for Halifax Regional Police on my father's murder case, but had recently transferred to the R.C.M.P. and was now an Inspector. Initially, Kennedy and I had not hit it off at all, but we eventually became quite friendly.

It took several minutes for me to thread my way through the system, but eventually got through.

"Kennedy."

"Patrick. How are you?"

"Who's that?"

"It's me, Marc. Marc LeBlanc."

"Good God! Marc LeBlanc! I'll be damned. How have you been?"

"Fine. Married now. I think you knew that?"

"I did. Congrats. What can I do for you?"

"Do we have a problem with Neo-Nazis in Nova Scotia?"

"Neo-Nazis? No. Maybe a couple of nuts, but very few and isolated. However, we are keeping our eye on a group of Islamist extremists who, strange to relate, seem to be working closely with the Marxists."

"Members of the Communist Party?"

"It's hard to say. There are so many splits and splinter groups, few of them more than a handful of people. Marxists, Marxist-Leninists, Trotskyites, even Bakuninists...you name it."

"Are these people all anti-Semitic?"

"Are they ever! Virulent Jew haters, the lot of them. Jew hatred is what binds them. Otherwise it would be hard to find common ground. Why do you ask?"

"A good friend of mine who is Jewish recently received an anonymous anti-Semitic note."

"Where does he live?"

"She. Near Wolfville."

"Ah. Any connection with Acadia?"

"Yes, indirectly."

"There is a group there which we believe is responsible for some fairly nasty stuff. I don't mean bombs and assassinations, but disgusting propaganda."

"Patrick, would any of these people—even though they are not Nazis themselves—have any sympathy with the Nazis?"

"This is the damnedest thing. The Marxists wouldn't ever admit to having anything to do with the Nazis, but their allies, the Islamists, are great fans of Hitler, but think he didn't go far enough."

"You're joking. Really?"

"Yes, the Grand Mufti of Jerusalem during WWII was a guy called Mohammed Amin al-Husseini, who met with Hitler on a number of occasions and even helped to raise Muslim regiments for the Nazis in the Balkans. He knew all about the Holocaust and approved of it. These loonies at Acadia worship his memory."

"We just have one note so far. If she gets any more, or if we identify who sent them, I'll let you know."

"Please do. But, Marc, watch how you go. These fruitcakes could be dangerous."

Leslie was already seated at the Bistro when I arrived. He passed me a list containing the names of those who shared the residence with him:

Ronald Rankin	Frederick Umawayo
Joseph Mombourquette	Samir Al Ghussain
Jamil Shaath	Waleed Abu Ezam
William Shaw	Mahmoud Nusaybah

"Do you know where they are from, Leslie?"

"Rankin and Momberquette are from Nova Scotia. Shaw is from

Ontario. Umawayo is from South Africa. The others are from Jordan and Gaza."

"Do you hear any anti-Jewish talk around the house?"

"Sometimes, but they are pretty guarded when I'm about."

"Let me know if you overhear any more of it."

"Okay. Will do."

"And please change your password and keep your computer where nobody else can get at it."

"Right, I will. What happened, Marc?"

"Keep this to yourself, but Rachel got an anti-Semitic note, and my contacts at the RCMP tell me there is—for want of a better word—a cell of extremists here at Acadia."

"Holy crap."

"It looks as if they, or at any rate some of them, think our friend Dieter was a good guy and that we should lay off him."

"Hard to imagine. Do you want to come up and see the house?"

"Why not? I doubt if any of them would leave incriminating material lying around, but you never know."

I left the car and strolled back with Leslie to Highland Avenue. The house was a very large, three-storey affair with a more recent addition tacked on to the rear. Inside it was exactly what you would expect a student residence to be: untidy. We wandered around, but there was nothing particularly interesting on view.

Then we went upstairs. On the first landing there was a door with a poster of Che Guevara, another with Karl Marx and a third with Yasser Arafat.

We climbed higher, to the second landing. Here a door had a poster promoting Zululand, which bore a dramatic photograph of an elephant's closed eye. The other two doors were unadorned.

"This is my room," Leslie said, indicating the further door.

He unlocked it and we entered, stooping slightly because the ceiling was low. The bed was against one wall and a dresser and a clothes rack against the other. Under the dormer window was a table on which Leslie had spread material left behind in Eugen Dieter's strong box.

"Leslie," I said sternly, "you mustn't leave this stuff where somebody could find it. The lock on your door would be child's play to open."

I took out my wallet and handed him a hundred dollars. "Go get some kind of lockbox in town today."

"Sorry, Marc. I didn't think the material would prove so sensitive. I'll do as you suggest."

I looked at the table again and noticed the photograph of Dieter. Now it was in full light. When we had seen it at Ray's house, the light had been dimmer.

I picked it up and stared at a corner. "What's this little mark?" I asked Leslie.

"Where? I didn't notice any mark."

"Here." I took out my pen and pointed.

"Oh yeah. It looks like a number."

"Fuck me!" I exclaimed.

"What?"

"A number?"

"Well, a number that's backwards."

"Exactly. Backwards. That means the negative was the wrong way round, and so was the print!"

"So?"

"So, this guy is really holding the gun to his left shoulder. Which means he is right-handed."

"Shit!"

"We've got the wrong man. This isn't John Bland at all."

"Damn!" said Leslie.

"Yes. The man we want is Walter Klemper. Walter E. Klemper!"

Jeremy Akerman

20

Rosalie and I had smoked salmon, cream cheese, sliced tomatoes, cucumbers, and capers with bagels for breakfast the next day. The combination of flavours was not one I really liked, and especially because I much prefer hot breakfasts, but it was a great favourite of Rosalie's. With it I served some of the special Black Ivory coffee, a distinct, alluring beverage from Thailand's Golden Triangle.

When we had finished eating, I broke the bad news about our mistake with Eugen Dieter.

"You're joking!"

"No. We jumped to conclusions, largely because of Dieter's first name."

"But the alternative was Walter."

"Walter E. I'll bet the middle name will turn out to be Eugen."

"If it doesn't, we'll really be up the creek."

"If that happens, I don't know what we would do. Anyway, Leslie is starting work on Major Klemper today. We might have a report from him by tonight."

I paused, then said: "There's something else..."

"Oh? That sounds ominous."

"Rachel wants to keep it from Ray, but I don't see how we can indefinitely."

"What is it? What are you talking about?"

I told her about the note, my conversation with Inspector Kennedy and the information I received from Leslie.

"Poor Rachel. Though, from what I've heard, being called a 'Jew bitch' is mild in comparison with some anti-Semitic insults."

"You're right. I took a look on the internet, and some of the stuff is hair-raising. Stealing babies comes up time and again, and allegations that Jewish women have sex with dead bodies."

"Ugh!"

"Do you know any of these?" I asked, passing Leslie's list to her across the table.

"I don't recognize the others, but I do know two of them. Mahmoud Nusaybah is one. He was a history major."

"What's he like?"

"Quiet unless provoked. Then he can get nervous and excitable, with a runaway mouth."

"About what?"

"Palestine. Jews. Refugee camps. That whole shmear."

"Do you think he could be a member of an extremist group?"

"I'm not sure. But this character certainly could." She pointed to William Shaw's name. "I'm convinced this guy is dangerous. He is a fanatic, but is charming and persuasive. He has a way of sucking weaker people into his orbit."

"Have you heard him express any anti-Semitic sentiments?"

"No, but he's too smart for that. He confines himself to very rational-seeming arguments as to why capitalism is about to collapse. Rational, that is, until you examine his premises."

"Does he socialize with the Arabs on the list?"

"Like I said, I only know those two, but wherever Shaw goes, Nusaybah is not far behind."

"Interesting. But short of getting a confession I doubt we'll ever know who sent the note to Rachel."

"Unless Leslie could compare the handwriting with stuff his house mates had written."

"Maybe. I'll ask him to surreptitiously keep a look out."

"Marc, you know if you want to have a look at William Shaw, he and his comrades are having a meeting tonight"

"Really? Where?"

"In a room in the Student Union building."

"Who is sponsoring the meeting?"

"I saw a poster for it. I think they call themselves Marxist-Leninist anti Revisionist post Maoists."

"You're putting me on."

"No. It was something like that. Apart from Shaw himself and maybe one or two others, I gather they are a bunch of nutters."

"Why don't we go?"

"If you're up for it, so am I. But let's not wear anything expensive, and do not take the Bugatti!"

"No, indeed. Let's take your Fiat and park it a few blocks away from the meeting."

When we got to the Student Union building and found the meeting room, the attendance was far bigger than we expected. There were some twenty very scruffy men, all with beards; a dozen or so good-looking women severely dressed; ten people whose gender was not immediately apparent; and seven or eight young men who could have been of Middle Eastern origin. There was a small desk at the front of the room and a large quantity of collapsible steel chairs.

Rosalie and I sat at the very back and tried to be as inconspicuous as possible.

For some minutes there was a general milling about and deafening sound of people all talking at the same time. Then a man got up and addressed the meeting. Rosalie leaned across to me and whispered, "That's Shaw."

"Comrades," he said, "The meeting will come to order."

"Hold on a minute," someone shouted. "Who appointed you the chairman?"

This was greeted by cheers of approval.

"It doesn't have to be me," said Shaw, somewhat taken aback.

"Who says we've got to have a chairman?" The voice shouted again.

"Structure is a tool of the capitalist oppressors," someone else cried.

There were more cheers and applause.

"No structure! Down with structure!" a harsh female voice called.

"No structure!" the crowd joined in.

"And why all these chairs?" A person of indeterminate gender demanded. "Chairs are the symbols of structure and the essence of oppression!"

"Away with the chairs!" cried one of the bearded men, and hurled his chair against the wall with a crash. Others followed suit until a pile of chairs had accumulated against a side wall.

Rosalie and I hastily sprung from ours as they were grabbed by two of the Middle Easterners and thrown across the room.

"No structure means freedom!" declared a tiny woman with purple hair.

"Comrades! Please!" Shaw cried. "Comrades, we have an important agenda."

"What agenda? We haven't approved an agenda!" This came from a fellow in the corner who was almost as wide as he was tall.

"Imposition of agenda from above is Fascism!" an older woman in a long earth-coloured dress exclaimed.

"Down with Fascism!" the crowd roared.

"But comrades," Shaw persisted, "we have to pass a resolution calling on the university to ban all activity by the Zionist capitalist scum!"

This quietened the room somewhat, and several of the people who were on the point of leaving, turned back.

"Down with the Zionist scum!" came a shout. This was greeted by loud cheers.

"Down with the capitalist conspiracy of Jew bankers and their lackeys and running dogs!"

"Hear! Hear!"

Shaw called for order so he could read out the motion. It took a few seconds for him to be heard. His voice was clear and histrionic.

"Resolved that we demand that the University immediately divest itself of all endowments, investments and others in any way connected with Zionist criminals. Further resolved that we demand that the University prohibit any meetings or speakers advancing the pernicious ideas of Zionism and Capitalism!"

The roar of approval was almost ear-splitting. People started raising their fists in a salute to the ceiling. Shaw's voice could just be heard under the din. "Motion carried! Unanimously! Meeting is adjourned."

Rosalie and I beat a hasty retreat and got out to the street before the crush. Someone was standing by a tree ahead of us.

"Jesus. That was quite something wasn't it?" It was Leslie.

"Leslie! Were you in the meeting? We didn't see you."

"I was standing by the door. I wanted to be sure of having a quick getaway."

"What an experience," said Rosalie. "I don't think I've ever come across such a disputatious crowd."

"But they all came together quickly to attack Jews," I said.

"Yeah, I noticed that," said Leslie. "I checked, and all the guys on that list were in the meeting, except Umawayo, Rankin and Mombourquette."

"Really? Well, that just tells us you must exercise greater care in future. And I don't just mean the materials and your computer."

"Yeah. That's what I was thinking, too," Leslie said soberly. "I wouldn't put anything past those lunatics."

21

Leslie called me early to say that he would be prepared to give us a report in the evening. I suggested that Ray and Rachel should pick him up and that they all come here to dinner. I thought I would cook the goose I bought at Harold Aikens' farm.

"Are you sure?" Leslie seemed uncertain.

"Why shouldn't I be?"

"I'm not exactly elegant company for snooty occasions."

"My dinners are not snooty occasions! Do you like goose?"

"I don't know. I've never had it."

"Well, this will be your opportunity to try it."

"Do I have to wear a suit?"

"Chump! Of course you don't. But you do have to wear socks and a shirt."

"Okay, then. You'll let me know if I use the wrong knife and fork."

"Don't be an ass!"

"Marc, I can tell you now that Walter Klemper is our man. I'll give you details tonight."

Rosalie came down as I was hanging up on Leslie, and asked me to make a breakfast I had told her about which I had once at Boisdale in London.

I had some black-backed gulls' eggs which I got from some youngsters who regularly scale the cliffs at Cape Split. With these I would make an omelette which I would then fill with lobster and crab, Italian truffles, and fresh, tender asparagus.

It was a bit fiddly to make, but was well worth the effort. The fact that Rosalie thought the breakfast was bliss was reward enough for me.

"What shall we do today?" She asked as she nursed her coffee.

"If you approve, I thought we should take a run down to St. Croix to see where the *Feinste* landed Klemper in 1942."

"What a good idea. I've never been there."

"Okay. But first I must take the goose out of the freezer. If I put it in cold water it should have thawed by the time we get home."

"How will you cook the goose?"

"I'll rub it with five-spice powder, salt, pepper and ground, dried orange peel, stuff it with prunes, walnuts and sausage meat, and slow roast it. I'll serve it with wild rice and creamed red cabbage. Does that sound alright?"

"Instead of the five-spice powder, use star anise."

"Sure, if you want. I think that would work."

"What shall we have as a starter?"

"Let's keep it simple and have smoked salmon with dill and capers."

"Lovely. And dessert?"

"I'll leave that to you."

"Okay. I'll pick up some fresh fruit on our journey today. Have you decided on the wines?"

"Yes. I think a Domaine du Closel, Clos du Papillon, Savennieres 2001 with the salmon and a 1989 Barolo Sperss, from Angelo Gaja, to go with the goose. You can go to the cellar and choose the one you want to go with the fruit."

~

We arrived in St. Croix Cove fifty minutes later and found it to be a delightful spot with a romantic waterfall, a quiet cemetery and a rocky foreshore. We could easily imagine the *Feinste* creeping along the coast in the dead of night and disgorging its dinghy containing SS Major Klemper.

His eight-kilometre trek across more or less open ground to Paradise, however, would have been arduous, especially if he were loaded down with equipment. We wondered if Hermann Hempel would have been expecting him and, if so, would he have signalled with a flashlight to indicate his location to Klemper?

Regardless of what a heartless beast this man must have been, Rosalie and I were forced to concede that his actions involved a great deal of courage and determination.

We walked around the area for about an hour, then, concluding there was nothing more we could discover, we headed back home, stopping on the way to buy some fresh fruit and vegetables at one of the numerous roadside markets.

The others arrived at six-thirty and, once they were installed in arm chairs in the living room, I served some 2005 Bollinger Vieilles Vignes Françaises Blanc de Noirs, an intriguing wine still carrying a lively bubble. We all sat back and savoured the Champagne while Leslie struggled with his backpack and laid out his many notes on the coffee table.

"Okay, folks. I guess I should begin at the beginning. Ray, your grandfather was almost certainly one Walter Eugen Klemper, born in the village of Blaibach, Bavaria in 1914 or 1915. The records say 1914, but if he was 80 when he died it would have been 1915. His parents were Helga and Klaus Klemper, apparently native Bavarians. Helga was the younger sister of Herman Hempel, who had emigrated to Canada in 1910."

Leslie told us that Walter was educated locally and then in the nearby, larger town of Bad Kotzting. Some time in the period following 1920, Walter was sent to Canada to stay with his uncle, Hermann Hempel, for a year, maybe two. On his return, he studied first at Regensburg University, served his compulsory six months in the Labour Service Corps, and then took medicine at Heidelberg University. He graduated in 1934. But then served his deferred military service for two years.

In 1939 he applied for and was inducted into the SS. Two years later, now with the rank of *Hauptsturmfuherer*, he was assigned to Ravensbruck Camp, where he became an assistant to Dr. Franz Gebhardt, who was eventually one of the 31 people convicted in the infamous 'Doctors' Trial' at Nuremberg.

Before the war, Gebhardt was an expert in the field of sports medicine. He wrote articles on physical medicine and rehabilitation and a textbook on sports rehabilitation, and was the senior doctor for the German Olympic team in 1936. Among his distinguished patients were Reinhardt Heydrich and Albert Speer. When he went to Ravensbruck, Gebhardt conducted experiments on inmates by breaking their legs and infecting them with various organisms in order to prove that the drugs currently in use for treating gas gangrene were inefficacious. He also attempted to transplant the limbs from camp victims to German soldiers wounded on the Eastern Front, with horrible results.

Klemper, with Gebhardt's encouragement and under his overall supervision, specialized in two areas of experimentation. One was trying to discover a method of induced premature aging, especially by attempting to infect inmates with progeria. It was then thought to be a genetically transmitted condition, but Klemper believed it could also be transmitted by transferring fluids from the affected to the unaffected. These efforts often resulted in patients dying. His other area of research was in conducting tests to see how long people could endure extreme deadly pain before actually expiring.

As was the case with Eugen Dieter, details about his transfer to Foreign Intelligence Department Six were hazy, but if he volunteered it seems there must have been a reason why Ravensbruck would let him go. Gebhardt was getting into trouble with the Nazi leadership for his many failures, so maybe Klemper was thought to be associated with Gebhardt's failures and was transferred as a punishment.

Leslie then reeled off a timeline:

"1942, aboard the U-boat *Feinste*, Klemper was brought to Canada, where he landed at St. Croix Cove and may have taken refuge with his uncle, Herman Hempel.

"1943, after a mysterious, prolonged visit to Halifax, he returned to Paradise and started to practice medicine with Dr. Henry Wilkinson.

"1944, he set up his own practice and bought a small house.

"1945, he married Ida Murchison.

"1946, their first child, Hilda, was born, and Klemper moved his residence to Port Williams. Hilda died in 1959.

"1947, their second child, a boy, was born. This was Ray's Uncle Oscar, who died in 2019.

"1948, Ray's father, Edgar, was born.

"1949, their final child, Heather, was born."

Leslie looked up to check that we were following, then went back to his notes. "Within two years of their births, both Hilda and Heather showed signs of progressive progeria. Neither lived beyond her thirteenth birthday. Heather died in 1962, and Ida died in1968.

"Over the next decade, Klemper, now John Bland, developed a reputation for quality landscapes which he painted largely on family camping holidays around the province. In 1978 Bland was severely injured in a car accident and was confined to a wheelchair for the remainder of his life. He died in 1995, aged 80 or 81, depending on which date you choose."

"That's very comprehensive," said Ray. "Thank you very much for a job well done."

"There's more, I'm afraid. It's not nearly as nice." Leslie sounded cautious, apprehensive.

"Why don't we leave that until after dinner?" Rosalie said.

"Good idea!" Rachel exclaimed. "Any more of those Nazis would ruin my appetite."

At dinner the conversation turned to other subjects, not all of them of a lighter nature. Rachel told us that she had informed Ray of the anti-Semitic note and that, while infuriated, he had not—as she put it—"lost it." She raised this now, she said, because she had received another such note only today, but this time it was more explicit.

Rosalie and I related our adventures the previous day at the meeting, with Leslie providing colour commentary.

"When they started throwing chairs at the wall, I got really nervous," Rosalie said.

"I think most of them are loonies with nothing better to do with their time," said Leslie, "but it seems to me there is a hard core of serious fanatics who could be trouble."

"That's my opinion, too," I said, "and if Leslie doesn't think it could expose him to any danger, I'm going to pass on a few names to my friend in the RCMP."

"Be my guest," said Leslie.

I cleared away the plates from the smoked salmon and checked the goose, which had been resting for some time. The cabbage was ready and the rice was done, so I poured the Barolo and then carved the meat.

I had doubts about the combination, but it all seemed to work well.

When Rosalie served her assorted fruit she nearly gave me a heart attack by producing a bottle of Chateau D'Yquem 1959. It was the only bottle I had of this fabled vintage and was worth over $3,500.

Unspeakable Evil

I was about to remonstrate with her that this was entirely the wrong occasion for it, but I saw she had already opened it, so I said nothing. In the event, it was fabulous and prompted many 'ooh's and 'ahh's around the table.

Then we returned to the living room, where Rosalie served coffee. I offered our friends Cognac, but everyone was still nursing the extraordinary Yquem. This was Leslie's cue to produce his notes.

"If it's all the same to you I won't read it in German, and I won't translate all the notes word for word. The relevant ones start when Hilda is two, and record his eagerness to see if she develops progeria—as he obviously hopes she does."

He paused for several seconds. "I'm sorry folks, there's no way I can dress this up. I wish I could."

"Go on Leslie," said Rachel. "We all understand what we are letting ourselves in for."

"Well, okay. Some months later, when Hilda does show symptoms of the disease, Eugen is almost ecstatic. A few years later, when Heather also develops symptoms, he is triumphant. There's no other word for it."

"The swine!" Ray cursed.

"The notes over the next decade detail the various concoctions he feeds the girls and the so-called treatments he administers."

"What do you mean 'so-called'?" I asked.

"Some of the things he tried sound more like medieval witchcraft than medicine. At several points, he actually bleeds the girls."

"He bled them?" Rachel was aghast.

"Yes, and injected them with all kinds of chemicals. I don't recognize many of them. You can check them out for yourself if you want. The ones I did recognize I looked up on the internet and found that none of them would have been pleasant for the girls, and some of them would have been exquisitely painful."

"Christ!" Ray cried. "My own grandfather was a monster!"

"It would appear so. What's worse is that, when Hilda died, he doubled down on the experiments on Heather. The last few years of her life must have been a living hell."

"My God!" Rosalie blanched.

"For me, the most appalling thing these notes make clear is that when each of his daughters dies, he expresses no remorse at all. In fact, he seems to be mad at them for somehow letting him down. Please don't ask me to read them again. I actually threw up when I first read some of them. If you want to check my translation with someone else, I won't be offended."

"Thank you, Leslie. That's good of you," Ray said.

"Tell me, Leslie, do the notes, at any point, indicate how Ida reacted to all this?" Rosalie asked.

"No, but I get the strong impression from the way he writes that Ida and the boys were kept away, first from their elder sister and then from the younger."

"What do you mean?"

"Sort of kept separate. They lived separate lives."

"Like prisoners?"

"Yes. And I also got the impression that if his wife was not actually a weak-minded woman, he certainly regarded her as such."

"No wonder Dad would never talk about him," said Ray. "Even if the boys were kept well away from what was clearly the torturing of their sisters, they must have known that all was not normal."

"Not surprising that he left home as soon as he could," Rachel added.

We sat there in silence, which persisted as each of us looked at the floor, the ceiling, anywhere but at each other.

Finally, Leslie rose, gathered up his things and went to the door. Ray and Rachel followed.

Rosalie and I watched them go without another word.

22

When we got up in the morning, Rosalie and I were still subdued, almost numbed, by what we had heard the night before from Leslie. We desperately wanted to believe there had been some mistake—maybe an error in translation—because, although we were familiar with Nazi atrocities, this was the first time we had been brought face to face with an actual perpetrator. The thought that a father could so cruelly exploit his own children for wickedly perverted, pseudo-scientific purposes was an assault against logic and all sense of decency.

Yet we knew it was, must be, true. All that remained for us was to discover if Walter Klemper—alias John Bland—had committed any further obscenities following the wretched demise of his two daughters, or whether, perhaps in contrition, he had turned his hand to the benign pursuit of landscape painting, somehow hoping to redeem himself.

In an attempt to cheer us up, I cooked some home-made sausages for breakfast. The humble sausage looks easy enough to make, yet its preparation is riddled with pitfalls. First, the mix has to be of the right proportions: too little fat is a common mistake that results in sausages that are too dry; too much rusk (or toasted breadcrumbs) can also make them dry; too coarse a grind is unpleasant to the tongue.

Then there is the seemingly simple matter of getting the meat into the casings. This can be a nightmare, even with the proper

Jeremy Akerman

equipment, if the casings are artificial (as opposed to natural intestines), or if they are too dry or too wet.

If all has gone well up to this point, casings still have a bad habit of bursting in the pan, even if one has made the compulsory fork pricks in the skin. Suffice it to say, given all the difficulties, that sausage-making is something I seldom do. But when it is done right, with fresh pork shoulder and fat in as fine a mince as possible and subtly seasoned with salt, pepper and nutmeg, it is a joy to behold.

Today the gods were with me, and the bangers were excellent. We ate them with a tad of hot mustard and lots of fresh bread and butter.

One of the many things Rosalie and I have in common is our belief that sausages must be accompanied by tea, not coffee, so this morning I made a large pot of Teguanyin. This is an oolong, a semi-oxidized tea originating in Fujian Province in China. One of its delicious assets is that it can be infused a number of times without developing bitter flavours.

After breakfast I put in a call to Inspector Kennedy.

"Twice in one week," he said. "Marc, I am greatly blessed."

"Patrick, I wanted to pass on some names to you. These people are at, or associated with, Acadia and are known anti-Semites who, in my opinion, are capable of extreme or violent acts."

"Okay, shoot. Is it a long list?"

"No. Just five names. Jamil Shaath, William Shaw, Samir Al Ghussain, Waleed Abu Ezam, Mahmoud Nusaybah."

"Ah, Bill Shaw. We know all about him. He's been on our radar for quite some time. A very unsavoury character. I've never heard of any of the others."

"Apparently, their antipathy is based in their belief that Jews have usurped Israel and that it should be handed over to them."

"Have you actually seen any of these guys in action, Marc?"

"Rosalie and I went to one of their meetings. It was wild. They are vituperatively anti Jew."

"Did you get the impression that they could be planning something out of the ordinary?"

"I can't say I did, Patrick, but I wouldn't put much past these guys, especially if Shaw is whipping them up."

"I see. Did your friend get any more *billets doux*?"

"Yes, she did. I didn't see it but she says it was foul."

"Okay. If she gets any more, ask her to give me a call."

"I will. Thanks Patrick."

"Oh, there's one more thing."

"Yes?"

"We got a call from the Art Gallery of Nova Scotia, saying that they suspected one of their paintings might be a forgery. They told my sergeant that you had been asking questions about the same painter."

"John Bland, yes."

"Another adventure?"

"On behalf of a friend who asked me to find out about his grandfather."

"The grandfather. Was he John Bland?"

"Yes."

"And have you found out anything?"

"Yes, I have. Far too much, in fact."

"Oh?"

"Turns out he was a Nazi spy landed here by sub in WWII."

"Marc, how do you get involved in these things? You don't wait for trouble to come to you. You go looking for it."

"Yeah. I know."

"Is there any connection between Mr. Bland and your friend who is getting the poison pen letters?"

"Yes. She is the fiancée of the grandson."

"Wow." Patrick whistled. "That must be a little uncomfortable."

"A little. Who was your man talking to at the Art Gallery?"

"Just a second, I've got it here somewhere…yes, Jerry Swift."

"He's the one I met with. What's the painting in question, do you know?

"Yes, it's called *Gathering Storm, near Fort Lawrence*."

"That was one of the paintings my friend recently donated to the gallery. Did they say why they suspect it?"

"Something about overpainting. Or was it underpainting. I don't know. Look, Marc, I have to go I am OIC on a murder case."

"I hope this one'll be more successful than my father's case," I said, a little bitterly.

"Ouch!" said Patrick. "We never closed that case, you know, Marc."

"I just wish we had caught whoever killed him."

"The guy is somewhere in Russia. And is likely to stay there."

"I know."

"Just tell your friend he'll be getting a visit from CATFPA fairly soon."

"Don't tell me it will be Frank Wilberforce!"

"Yes. You know Frank?"

"Yes…"

"Now, I must scoot. See you Marc."

I did know, and liked, Frank Wilberforce. He had been the agent from the Canada Art Theft and Forgery Prevention Agency who had investigated my father and his nefarious business following his still-unsolved murder. Wilberforce was noted for his knowledge, cunning, size, and gargantuan appetite, having once put away the equivalent of three breakfasts at my house.

No sooner had I hung up when the telephone rang. It was Fred Moody, the locksmith in New Minas.

"Marc, great news."

"What's it all about, Fred?"

"I've just had a call from my brother, George, who says he can make the alterations to Ray's attic on Friday, weather permitting."

"And will he be there the following day to put it all back the way he found it?"

"'Course he will!"

"How about the crane from your wife's cousin?"

"Get with the program, Marc. George couldn't get up to do the work without the crane, could he?"

"No, I guess not."

"Willy will be there with his 2.5 Carry Deck. First thing. Bright and early."

"Is Albert okay to bring his oxyacetylene kit?"

"Yes. I've asked him to come mid-afternoon. George should have safely removed and lowered the safe by then."

"And if the weather is bad?"

"If it's just spitting we'll be alright, but if there's a real downpour we'd have to put it off."

"Until when?"

"Dunno. 'Till whenever George next has a couple of free days I guess."

"Okay. Many thanks, Fred. I'll pass this along to Ray."

Jeremy Akerman

23

I called Ray the next day and told him to prepare himself for a major disruption in his life this coming Friday. It would involve literally bashing a hole in his roof and attaching cables from the crane to the safe, dragging the safe to the edge, then lowering it to the ground. There, Albert would use the oxyacetylene to cut the safe open and presumably dispose of the empty vessel once Ray had cleared out its contents. Then, the following day, George would set about repairing the hole in the roof.

It seemed an extraordinary way to go about accessing the safe's contents, but there was no other option. We could be certain, however, that whatever was in the safe had not been touched since 1978, when John Bland had sustained his injury in the car accident and could no longer mount the stairs to the attic.

"Oh, Ray, I was talking to my detective friend yesterday and he says there is some problem with one of the paintings you gave to the Art Gallery."

"Yes, I know," he replied. "I just had a call from a Frank Wilberforce, who says he is coming by the dealership to discuss it with me."

"Today? That's good. I know Frank. He's a good guy. Could I be there, too?"

"Sure. He said he would come around eleven."

I got to Ray's dealership exactly as Frank Wilberforce drove in. The contrast between my Bugatti and his rusty, old Ford could not have been greater.

It took him some time to extricate his bulk from the car, but when he did he was smiling from ear to ear. "Marc LeBlanc! I should have known you would be involved in this matter! How are you, old friend?"

"I'm fine, Frank. You look like your usual self."

"Is this another 'case' for you, Marc?" He asked with a laugh.

"Yes, I'm working on something for Ray Bland. I don't know, but it may be connected to this painting."

"That's okay by me. Let's go in."

We gathered in Ray's office, where we sat and his assistant served us with coffee. Frank mopped his brow with a large red handkerchief and took some notes from his briefcase.

"It's about that painting you donated to the Gallery, *Gathering Storm near Fort Lawrence*."

"Yes. It's by my grandfather. What's the problem with it?"

"I gather you can guarantee its provenance. That is, there's no question he painted it?"

"I don't think so. Until recently, it has been in a closet ever since he died in 1995. You were there when I took it out, Marc. What happened before that, I have no idea."

"I see," Frank said thoughtfully. "Was it on its own, or in company with other works?"

"There were a number of paintings, all together gathering dust in the back of the closet."

"So, there doesn't seem to be any reason why he would store somebody else's painting with his own?"

"None at all. Why would he do that? Besides, you can tell at a glance he did it."

"I'm inclined to agree. But the curator at the gallery thought there might be a question of forgery."

"That would be Jerry Swift?" I butted in.

"That's him. Quite a character." Frank rolled his eyes. "I'll tell you what this is all about. Apparently the gallery does a kind of x-ray of every acquisition to see if there is only one image represented."

"That wasn't the case here?"

"No. Originally the painting showed the shadows from the trees to be very long, indicating that it was late in the day, but someone—presumably your grandfather—painted over that section of the work to make the shadows much shorter."

"Indicating that it was done much earlier in the day," I said.

"Exactly. Not that there's anything wrong with that. Artists do that all the time. Some great and famous works have been discovered lurking under the surface of unpretentious mediocrities."

"So, my grandfather probably didn't like the painting as it was and changed it. I don't see that as a big deal."

"Nor do I, frankly. If this was some multi-million dollar Van Gogh I could understand the degree of caution, but for a Nova Scotia landscape it seems excessive. No offence intended. I didn't mean to suggest that your grandfather's work was inferior."

"None taken," said Ray. "What is it worth, incidentally?"

"I figure it would fetch about $5,000 at auction."

"Wow! That much?"

"Give or take. I don't think there is a case to be made for forgery, so I will advise Mr. Swift—"

"Doctor Swift," I corrected.

"Yes, Doctor Swift! I will advise Dr. Swift that he can go ahead and hang the painting without any worries."

"In its original form, or its final version?" I was curious.

"If Mr. Bland has given it to them as a gift, they can choose whichever version they prefer. Thank you for your time, Mr. Bland."

"I'll see you on Friday, Ray, around nine."

"It'll be a big day," Ray said.

Frank raised his eyebrows as if to ask for an explanation, but it was none of his business, so I said nothing and walked out into the sunshine with him.

"I was sorry to hear about your brother," Frank said.

"What?" It took me by surprise and, at first, I could not think what he was talking about. For a second I wondered if Larry had been caught.

"I heard your brother died. Please accept my condolences?"

"Oh yes. Thanks. He died somewhere abroad."

"Somewhere abroad?"

"Yes, in Italy. I hadn't seen him for many years."

"Still, it is sad. Losing your only brother."

"Yes. Very sad."

I felt uncomfortable lying about my brother to Frank, or to anyone, for that matter, but I could see no alternative. I could hardly admit that Larry was alive and kicking and the head of an international gang of criminals. Still less could I admit that I had seen Larry, very briefly, less than a year ago.

I think it was because I felt guilty about concealing the truth from Frank that I felt obliged to invite him to dinner. As expected, he accepted with alacrity.

"I hope you won't be offended if I don't fully appreciate your haute cuisine," he said. "You know I'm a steak and potatoes sort of guy."

"I'll make burgers. Will that suit you?"

"Down to the ground!" He laughed and rubbed his hands.

"And I'll be sure to make plenty. I remember what an appetite you have."

"What time?"

"Come about five."

Rosalie had come back in the mid-afternoon from the college, where she had been quietly digging around for signs of further activity from the anti-Semitic group. She found that several professors had received messages similar to the ones sent to Rachel because the senders, wrongly, thought their names sounded Jewish. English professor Eric Myers and Music professor Josh Murdoch, who had no Jewish connections, had foul notes placed on their desks.

I thought we had to tread very carefully in this matter, because I am a great believer in the freedom of speech, and the fact that something was nasty or unpleasant should not make it illegal. If something were said which was untrue, then the recipient could have recourse to libel and slander actions. I had always been uncomfortable with the notion of "hate crimes", believing that a crime is a crime, regardless of the motive behind it.

I felt very badly for Rachel, but somebody just saying they did not like Jews, or Christians, or Muslims, or New Yorkers, while stupid and bigoted, should not constitute a crime. If violence was threatened or incited, that was an entirely different matter; but just saying something unpleasant, or even disgusting, should be unrestricted by law.

I had no idea what Inspector Kennedy would do with the information I had passed to him, but I felt I had done my duty. I owed it to Rachel to have taken some action, but beyond that, I was not prepared to go much further. If Rosalie or Leslie discovered with certainty who had sent the notes, I thought that the most we should do would be to let the perpetrators know they had been unmasked, inform the university administration and then back away.

I told Rosalie of my reservations and, while she differed with me to some extent, she agreed that pursuing these anti-Semites was something which should be treated with caution.

Frank rolled up around five-twenty and deposited himself in the largest chair on the deck. I furnished him with a large glass of Chablis, and he and Rosalie discussed art and forgery while I prepared dinner.

I could overhear that Frank was telling her the fascinating story of the Dutch painter Van Meegeren, who sold a Vermeer to *Reichsmarschall* Hermann Göring during the Nazi occupation of the Netherlands. When, after the war, he was put on trial as a traitor and collaborator, he proved the painting was a forgery and was acquitted!

In the kitchen, I went about preparing what is, at best, a preposterously grotesque meal. My burgers are impossible to pick up and eat with one's hands because they are so large and so full of ingredients, but I knew that if anyone could do justice to them, it would be Frank Wilberforce.

First, I used extra-large buns, which I lightly toasted, and on the lower half of each I spread lots of English hot mustard. On the upper halves I put very thick layers of mayonnaise. On each of them I placed thick slices of ripe tomato, several slices of dill pickles and heaps of partly-fried onion. Then the meat patty (medium ground, because plenty of fat is essential) would go on each pile, then be topped by the upper half of the bun.

With these I served freshly boiled corn on the cob, with lashings of butter.

As predicted, Rosalie and I were hard-pressed to finish a burger each with two cobs of corn, but Frank had no trouble putting away three burgers and four corn cobs. We washed it down with several bottles of Morgon 2016, a sturdy wine, bursting with fruit, from one of the villages in Beaujolais. It was redolent of sunshine, rolling hills and quaint settlements with small churches.

We sat very happily under the slowly-sinking sun and listened to Frank regaling us with stories of great forgers, many of whom, at least for a while, got away with their crimes. He told us about British artist John Myatt, who went down in history as the man behind what Scotland Yard called 'the biggest art fraud of the 20th century'. He painted almost 200 forgeries, many of them sold by some of the biggest auction houses in the world, including Sotheby's.

Then there was the Hungarian painter Elmyr de Hory, who sold 1,000 paintings to galleries across the world, including forged Picassos, as well as counterfeit works allegedly by Degas, Matisse and Modigliani.

Frank's favourite was Wolfgang Beltracchi, who painted in the styles of famous artists when he was a teenager, having learned from his father, who was an art restorer. Instead of making copies, he made new works and sold them at flea markets. He particularly liked paintings in the style of Heinrich Campendonk, and fooled the leading scholar Andrea Firmenic. His work sold for astronomically high prices at auction, and his Campendonk painting *Landscape with Horses*, which was bought by the actor Steve Martin, went for $850,000.

If he had not fallen asleep in mid-sentence, I am sure Frank could have gone on all night. Since Rosalie and I could not possibly carry someone of his size to a bedroom, we fetched a warm duvet and wrapped it around him. It was not forecast to be a cold night, so we left him, snoring peacefully away.

We knew that, however well or ill he slept, we would have to provide a massive breakfast for him in the morning.

24

This was indeed going to be a big day, one on which we could not waste time lolling about over a lengthy breakfast, so I had prepared it the night before. I had cooked some hard boiled eggs, poached some salmon and had sliced some Serrano ham, so all that was needed was to take it from the fridge and brew some Blue Mountain coffee.

Unlike most people we knew, Rosalie I were inordinately fond of cold food, especially in summer time, and we remembered some treasured experiences of this kind of meal.

One was dinner on the side of a Scottish mountain, comprised Loch Ryan oysters; an exquisite, velvety Vichyssoise flaked with black truffles; a marvellous salad of lobster, langoustine; and oysters with fat, Vale of Evesham asparagus, quail's eggs and delicious home-made mayonnaise. As we sipped out Champagne, we watched the sun sink over the loch and, just as we were finishing our fresh raspberries and double cream, it disappeared behind the heather-covered braes. Somewhere in the distance, a lone piper played the lament for Mary MacLeod, *Mairi ni'n Alasdair Ruaidh*, composed by the great Patrick Òg MacCrimmon in the early 1700s.

We awakened Frank, who still had the dew on his duvet, and he rose like some kind of prehistoric beast and lumbered into the nearest bathroom. When he emerged, we told him we were in a hurry, explaining why he would not be getting a cooked breakfast. He seemed untroubled by this and proceeded to demolish a good half of everything on the table.

"Wonderful!" he proclaimed, wiping his face with his red handkerchief. "And do you know what? That was the best night's sleep I've had in years!"

"That's good," said Rosalie. "We were afraid the Boogey Man might get you in the night."

"He's welcome to try anytime." Frank laughed heartily. "Well, folks, I must love you and leave you."

We watched his car disappear and then locked up and climbed into the Bugatti.

When we arrived at Rachel and Ray's, there was a small army of people and vehicles in the yard and on the grass at one side of the house. It appeared that this would be one of the events of the year in Port Williams, as a small crowd had gathered on the sidewalk in front of the house, and a number of local children were hanging over the next-door fence.

The back tracks of the crane had knocked over and were crushing some day lilies and the lawn was churned up. Willy was looking nervous about the damage he had caused, and so too was Rachel, who stood with a drawn face, clearly wondering if all this would be worthwhile.

Fred was pretending to be in command, looking very important and barking orders, but George either ignored them or countermanded them with instructions of his own.

Albert was already there with his gas tanks on a trolley, even though he knew he would not be needed for hours. He laughed and explained to me that he came early because he did not want "to miss the excitement".

Ray was pacing up and down, having donned coveralls for the occasion, adding his own, equally ignored, commands in the general cacophony.

Rosalie, strangely fascinated by the chaos, had found a lawn chair and had made herself comfortable, determined to watch the spectacle from start to finish.

Rachel came up to me and suggested we go inside for coffee, surmising that nothing important would occur on the outside of the house any time soon. I agreed, so we threaded our way through the people and equipment and went in by the back door.

While she was making the coffee, I brought her up to date on investigations into the anti-Semitic group and how I had forwarded their names to Inspector Kennedy.

"The damnedest thing is, Marc, that 'Antisemitism' is really an inadequate term for hatred which targets Jews."

"How do you mean?"

"Well, since there is no such thing as 'semitism' it is difficult to be 'anti' it."

"I thought it was a real word meaning Semitic peoples."

"Yes, Semitic means relating to languages such as Hebrew, Arabic, Aramaic and Phoenician, but there's no such thing as 'Semitism'. The word 'antisemitism' was invented in the 19th-century Jew-hater Wilhelm Marr, who tried to disguise his bigotry with the false characteristic of race so he could appeal to people who liked defining things in pseudo-scientific terms."

"I didn't know that," I admitted.

"One of the problems is that so many think that Jew hatred is just another form of racism."

"Isn't it?"

"No. It's a uniquely paranoid and murderous mindset. The Jews are a unique people victimized by a unique prejudice. People assume that prejudice against Jews is against them as individuals, but Judaism is not like Christianity, where people make their own pact with God via their chosen denomination."

"I'm not sure I understand."

"Jewish religious identity is rooted in the land of Israel, where the Jews were historically the only people for whom it was ever their national kingdom. So, Israel is the very heart of Judaism. If you say the Jews have no right to the land of Israel, you are attacking Judaism itself."

"I'm afraid you've lost me."

"Saying you dislike Jews and wish they would get lost is generally regarded as bad, but nobody seems to have a problem if you say you hate Israel and wish it would disappear from the map."

"I notice some groups are saying that Jews are the apex of 'white privilege'," I said.

"That's preposterous, of course, and not only because many Jews are brown and black. The whole 'social justice' movement and identity politics are deeply rooted in anti-Jewish prejudice. The vicious stereotype of rich, powerful Jews oppressing the vulnerable has been an essential page in the left's handbook for years. That is why, in order to justify their bigotry, they have to portray Israel as a villain in the alleged fight against colonialism, imperialism and racism."

"Thanks, Rachel. I can't pretend I fully understand, but I am more clued in than I was before."

"Sorry to lecture you, Marc. We'd better go out and see the show."

George had made a much neater hole in the roof than I had expected and was now climbing from the bucket of the crane into the attic. He had attached chains to the bucket and, we assumed, was likewise fastening them around the safe.

His muffled voice could just be heard above the crane's engine. "Alright, Willy. Gently does it. Pull her out."

We could hear the heavy scrape on the wooden floor as Willy dragged the safe to the very lip of the opening.

"I'm going to need help to help me edge this great thing onto the bucket. Fred, Albert and Marc, get up here, you lazy buggers!"

We rushed into the house, scampered up the stairways to the attic and went forward to assist George, but even though the safe was still upright we could not budge it.

"Willy, she won't move," George called. "Could we lower her down by the chains?"

"Could, but she might swing, and if she did, whatever was in her way'd take an awful bashing."

"Yeah. I see that. Okay, Willy, can you get the teeth of the bucket under the front of the safe?"

"I can give her a try," said Willy. "Here goes."

Moving very slowly, Willy edged the bucket forward and, tearing into the floor planks, managed to get the teeth about six inches under the safe.

"That's as far as I can risk."

"Okay. Now guys we gotta shove her on bit by bit. First, let's swivel her to the left, then to the right."

With much puffing and grunting we eventually slid the safe onto the bucket. It looked extremely precarious.

"Now, Willy, as slow as you can," George called. "She's doing a balancing act right now."

Since even the smallest movements of the crane's arm were jerky, the safe teetered frequently as the bucket came down. Unfortunately, when it was about eight feet from the ground it tipped over and fell to the lawn with a sickening thud, burying itself several inches into the turf.

"The eagle has landed," said Rosalie, enjoying every minute.

"What now?" Ray asked. "Should we try to get her upright again?"

"No," said Albert rather like a surgeon, moving in after all preliminary preparations had been done. "It'd better if I was to take the top off anyway, so we may as well leave like that until I've opened her up."

"Yes. Alright, Albert."

"Get all this equipment out of here and have everyone moved back out of the way." Albert was now in unquestioned command.

We all did as we were told, except Fred, who, unwilling to accept a subordinate position, moved forward to stand by Albert.

"You too, Fred. Unless you got a helmet, goggles and gloves."

Fred, forced to concede he had none of the specified items, retreated, grumbling to himself.

"I don't want anyone standing around me," said Albert. "Could be dangerous. This is going to take at least half an hour, so you'd best go for a coffee or something."

The crowd dissipated, and Willy drove the crane away. George got into his truck and announced his departure, too.

Fred waved them goodbye and turned to Ray. "I've managed to keep it all below a thousand. That's a good price, considering. I'll take a cheque, if you don't have the cash."

"No, I don't carry a thousand dollars in cash. Make a back for me and I'll make out the cheque."

Fred bent over while Ray wrote the cheque. He examined it by holding it up to the light, then hopped into the truck and was gone.

The flame, sparks, smoke and smells coming from Albert's glowing torch drove us indoors where Rachel made fresh coffee.

"That's a big dent in your lawn," I said to Ray.

"Easy to fix. I'm in this thing to the end, regardless."

"I gather Albert is going to take the lid of the safe as if he were opening a can of beans." Rachel said.

"That's the idea, darling. It's obviously an old safe, so I doubt he will run into any internal counter-theft mechanisms, but unless he is as close to the top as possible, he might scorch or burn some of the contents."

"It would be a lot of trouble just for some ashes and embers."

"Indeed it would. Listen!"

"What?"

"No sounds! He must have finished. Should we troop out there, or does Albert want to make a grand entrance and bring the crown jewels to us in here?" Rosalie asked.

"I think we'd better wait and see," I said.

After several minutes we heard Albert wiping his shoes on the hall mat. To our acute disappointment he carried only a small diary.

"Is that it?" Ray asked. "All that for a little book?"

"No, there's also nine paintings in their frames. Nice ones, by the look of them. They was too heavy for me to carry."

"We'll go and look at them," I said. "I imagine they're dirty so we'll put them in the conservatory until we've cleaned them. May I have the book, Albert?"

"Sure. The writing is right tiny. And it's all in some foreign language."

"Ah, another job for Leslie." I said. "Let's go and take a look at the paintings."

When we were back on the lawn, Albert said, "Do you want me to cut it some more? It'll be a bugger to shift the size it is."

"Yes, thank you, Albert," said Ray, "I think that would be best."

"I'll even take the scrap off your hands, Ray."

"Sure, that would suit me fine. If you wouldn't mind, could you take out the paintings one by one, please?"

"Here we go. The littlest one first," said Alberta, extricating a painting and passing it to Ray.

I was surprised how clean the canvas was, but I thought that, apart from a little dust enclosed in the safe, it would not have attracted dirt in forty-five years.

"*Five Islands Provincial Park*, John Bland. June 10 1969." John read, "That's quite a nice one. Next, please, Albert."

"*Burntcoat Head Park. Noel Shore*. John Bland. July 31 1969.

163

Next.

"*Rawdon Gold Mines*. June 23. John Bland. 1970. Next.

"*Clyde River Campsite*. July 25. John Bland. 1970. Next.

"*Ben Eoin*. June 4 1972. J. Bland. Bit of a gap there. Wonder why? Next.

"*Seal Island Bridge*. August 2. 1973. J. Bland. Another gap. Next.

"*Grand Etang, Cabot Trail*. John Bland. June 21 1975.Next.

"*Bear River*. August 13. 1976. John Bland. 1976. Next painting please, Albert."

"'Taint actually a painting," said Albert. "'Tis this here piece of paper."

"Ah. An old friend. *Storm Clouds Gathering near Fort Lawrence*. John Bland. July 12 1977."

"Ray," Rosalie piped up. "Apart from the Fort Lawrence painting and these in the safe, all the others were just signed John Bland and the year. Why are these signed differently?"

"I don't know."

"And why was Fort Lawrence—obviously intended to be sealed in the safe—withdrawn from it prior to the committal?" I asked.

"Again, I have no idea." Ray looked pensive. "What would you say about the quality of these?"

"I think they are technically very good," said Rachel, "but they all have what I think you called 'an unfinished look,' Marc."

"Not unfinished exactly," I said, "but as if the last stages had been rushed. I don't know; it could all be my imagination."

"But didn't you say that Mr. Swift—?"

"Doctor Swift."

"—Doctor Swift agreed with you?"

'Yes, he did, but it's a strong possibility that neither one of us knows what we're talking about."

"Can we get anything from the chronology?" Rachel asked. "We have two paintings in '69, two in '70, nothing in '71, one in '73, nothing in '74, one in each of '75, '76 and '77."

"Of course, there were other paintings he did during that whole period," I said. "I remember Swift's list had quite a few of them. We should not forget that Bland was painting for only a relatively short time. From the time Ida died until his accident in 1978."

"Then what was different about these?" Rosalie asked. "Did he think these were special, extra good, and maybe too good for the common herd to own? After all, we know he was an arrogant son of a bitch."

"If that was the case, why did he remove Fort Lawrence from the bunch?" Ray demanded.

"Oh," Rachel said quietly, "I think we might find that in 1977 Bland had some pressing financial problems and had to hock the painting, but because it was important for some reason, he needed a record of it along with the eight in the safe."

"Yes! That makes sense."

"Can I go now?" Albert asked.

"Sorry, Albert. Yes, you can, and thank you very much for all your good work."

"Right," said Albert, not moving.

"What it is?" Ray asked.

"I was expecting a little fee, like."

"Fred said it was included in what I paid him."

"Ah, well, that's Fred all over, isn't it?"

"How much?" Ray sighed.

"Two hundred should cover it, seeing as it's you, Ray."

"Help me to put the paintings in the conservatory, please Marc. Then we should have some dinner. Rachel, do we have anything in the house?"

"Maybe a crust of dry bread, and a fine water."

25

The day after Albert opened the safe, Leslie called me. I recounted the previous day's events, and said I had the small diary for him to see. He told me that he had to go to Ottawa for a few days to do research for his doctoral thesis, but asked me to bring the diary into town where he would take a quick look at it.

Rather than risk an accident with the original, I decided to photo-copy the pages and let him take those.

He thumbed through them with an increasing frown.

"What's the matter? Isn't it German?" I asked.

"Yeah, I think so. But it is all in code which could take forever to figure out."

"Well, take it with you, and if you have a spare moment, see what you can make of it."

"Okay. I'll see you in four days' time."

~

As it happened, two days after this meeting both Rosalie and I tested positive for the Pirola strain of COVID-19, and suffered so badly we could hardly think straight, let alone move anywhere except from bed to couch. It was another five days before we could walk properly or leave the house. I had warned all our friends to stay well away from us for the duration, so we had little contact with the outside world.

It came as something of a surprise to receive in the mail an invitation to Ray and Rachel's wedding. In a hand-scribbled note with the invitation, Ray explained it had been a quick decision and that he wanted me to be his best man and Rosalie to be Rachel's Matron of Honour.

The wedding was to be held in the Court House in Kentville in three weeks and would be a civil ceremony conducted by Walter Bryden, who was a Justice of the Peace in addition to being a practising lawyer.

Of course, we were both delighted by this news, but recognized it would be something of a bittersweet experience for Rachel. Her marriage would not be recognized in her own faith because Ray was not a Jew and did not think he could take the necessary time to convert. However, Ray said, the blow would be softened by the presence of her friend, Rabbi Karlin from Halifax, as well as by a very old friend, Chedva Bensaid.

He also said that, if possible, there would be two very special guests at the wedding. We searched our minds but could not imagine who they could be.

~

It was some days after Rosalie and I had recovered from COVID that I heard from Leslie, who told me he had stayed in Ottawa longer than expected, researching the pre-war correspondence between Canada and Berlin. In particular, he said, he had turned up a great deal of new material indicating that Canadian Prime Minister MacKenzie King was an enthusiastic fan of Hitler. Leslie said that when King entered the Third Reich, he wrote that his meeting with the Fuhrer was the "the day for which I was born."

"Holy cow!" I said. "These anti-Semites are everywhere."

"Yeah. King was one of the worst. Pretty much kept the gates closed to Jewish immigration."

"Wasn't there a ship full of Jewish refugees whom King refused to allow in?"

"Yes, that was in May, 1939. The *St. Louis* was carrying more than 900 Jewish refugees. Canada refused to take them and the ship was forced to return to Europe. Of the 900, more than 250 *St. Louis* passengers were eventually killed in the Holocaust."

"The more you learn, the more disgusted you get."

"Ain't that the truth?"

"Did you get anywhere with the diary?"

He had not managed to crack the code, he said, and needed what he called 'corroborating factors' from another source. I confess I did not really understand him, but I gathered he meant that if information from somewhere else coincided with something in the diary it could lead to unravelling the mystery.

I urged him to keep trying, saying that we would meet the following weekend.

I went out onto the deck and looked at the distant vines starting to yellow. The harvest, at least of hybrid grapes, would be good this year, and I hoped I would get some return on my investment in John Dempster's winery.

I took a broom and had started to sweep a few leaves off the planking when a blood curdling shriek came from the living room. I rushed in, expecting Rosalie to have had a heart attack.

"What? What is it?"

"Marc, look! Look at this!" She swivelled the monitor so I could see it better. It was an item entitled 'Gone but Not Forgotten', dated June 2005. I read quickly, anxious to discover what had made my wife so excited.

> Some older residents of this sleepy little community of South West Margaree still talk about "their Rosie" thirty

years after the little girl's body was found drowned under mysterious circumstances. The community was shocked to its roots when the police could find no apparent explanation for the thirteen year old's body apparently having been repeatedly submerged. S. W. Margaree lies south of the famous Acadian communities of Grand Etang and Cheticamp.

"So what?"

"Grand Etang! That was where John Bland did one of his paintings."

"Jesus, you're right. When was it painted?"

"1975"

"Same year as the little girl's death!"

"You know who your next call must be, don't you?"

"Yes, Patrick Kennedy."

Right away, I called Patrick and arranged to meet him the following day at H Division Headquarters in Dartmouth.

"Glad to help, Marc, but can you tell me what this is all about?"

"It's about cold cases."

"Cold cases?"

"Yes, cases which were suspicious but where the perpetrator was never found."

"Oh, you mean unsolved cases?"

"Yes."

"Okay. Can you give me some parameters?"

"Between 1968 and 1978. Homicides."

"Right. See you at 1 pm."

Jeremy Akerman

26

As I was preparing to drive to Dartmouth to see Patrick Kennedy, a new, mid-level sedan pulled into the forecourt and disgorged a young man in his thirties. He wore a gray suit, brown shoes, and a blue shirt with an orange tie. He carried a black attaché case.

"Mr. LeBlanc? Marc LeBlanc?"

"Yes. Who are you?"

"I'm Sheridan McCall from the Department of Justice."

"Really? What can I do for you, Mr. McCall?"

"I was wondering if I might see your license. Only a formality, you understand."

"Sure," I said hesitantly, wondering what on earth this could be about. Had I unknowingly been involved in a traffic accident? I took out my wallet and extricated the license. "Here you go."

"No sir, this is your driver's license."

"Yes. What license do you want?"

"Your Private Investigator's License."

"My what? What are you talking about?"

"Am I to understand you have been undertaking work as a private investigator but without a license and without conforming to the provisions of Private Investigators and Private Guards Act, 1989 as amended 1992?"

"Since I have never even heard of any of that stuff, obviously I couldn't conform to it, and am not now, nor have I ever been, a private investigator."

"That is not our information," said McCall with a frown. "Do you deny that last year you led an investigation which resulted in the discovery of what has become known as 'the Holy Grail'?"

"Which I did entirely as a private citizen and for which I received no payment of any kind."

"And do you further deny that you are in the course of conducting an investigation into matters relating to one of Nova Scotia's best-known artists?"

"I am undertaking a few inquiries on behalf of a personal friend, related to his family. Again without any remuneration."

"You have been questioning strangers in their homes?"

"There is no law against my visiting and talking to any person who is willing to speak with me."

"No, not unless you misrepresent yourself?"

"I have never done so," I said.

My mind was racing. Surely to God a free citizen in Nova Scotia in 2024 was allowed to speak to whomever he wanted without Big Brother Government breathing down his neck. Had somebody connected with old Mrs. Ingraham complained? Or had it been the late George Zwicker's son? Or, had it been the pompous and prickly Swift—Doctor Swift—who had registered his objections?

And on what grounds would they have protested? Or was there a more sinister force behind this, a secretive group of anti-Semites who did not wish the dirty laundry of Walter Klemper to be aired?

"I have a copy of the Act here for you," said McCall, passing me a fairly thick, white package. "You will note that Section 25, subsection (1) states that 'Every person who violates Section 4 shall be guilty of an offence and liable on summary conviction to a penalty not exceeding five hundred dollars.'"

"And what the hell does Section 4 say?"

"Section 4 says that No person shall (a) engage in, carry on, advertise or hold himself out as carrying on the business or practice

Jeremy Akerman

of providing private investigators or private guards; or (b) act as a private investigator or private guard, unless he is the holder of a license therefor issued under this Act."

"This is a lot of nonsense!" I started to get angry and, had not Rosalie come out to find out what the commotion was about, I might have rammed McCall's Act somewhere he would have found most unpleasant.

"What's going on Marc?" she inquired.

"Some pettifogging bureaucrat trying to say we have been passing ourselves off as private detectives."

"Mrs. LeBlanc is also involved?" McCall said. "There are two of you in the business?"

"There is NO business!" I screamed at the man. It seemed to have registered, and he took a step back, looking slightly scared.

"I'm just doing my job, sir," he said in a subdued tone. "I'll leave you with the Act and would advise you to apply for a licence, otherwise—"

"Otherwise what?"

"Otherwise you never know what could happen."

He scurried to his car, and took off rather more speedily than our lane warranted.

"Is this serious?" Rosalie asked when he had gone. "Are we going to be in trouble?"

"I don't know. Call Walter Bryden and ask him if he'll see you today. If he will, take this Act and get his advice on it. I don't know how long I'll be in Dartmouth, but we can compare notes when I get back.

~

Patrick Kennedy's office in H Division Headquarters was quite different from the rather grimy corner of the city squad room where I had first met him, a little more than a year ago. The building was modern and smart, and his office was pleasant and airy, lighted by a large window.

Kennedy looked very happy behind his large steel desk, and I noticed he had lost weight. We shook hands, exchanged a few pleasantries then got down to business.

"First I need to know why you're making this kind of inquiry. It's not that the information is classified or anything like that, but the usual way of acquiring this information is by way of application and paying a fee. It would normally take you months to get it."

I started at the beginning and told him the whole story of how Rosalie and I had become involved, the remarkable discoveries we had made, and where our investigations now stood.

"Thank you," Patrick said. "That gives me exactly the reason I need for by-passing and fast-tracking."

"It does?"

"Something which could lead to the resolution of an unsolved crime gets a certain priority."

"Ah, yes, I see."

"What's the matter, Marc?"

"I'm hesitant to say too much at this stage, but it might—I repeat, *might*—lead to solving more than one crime."

"More than one?"

"Well, yes. Actually, maybe, possibly, as many as nine."

"Nine?" Patrick's eyes almost popped out of his head. "Wow!"

I nodded.

He took off his jacket and hung it on the back of a chair, loosened his tie and rolled up his shirt sleeves. "This is hard to believe, I'm sure you understand that, Marc. But let's get to it. You told me 'homicides' between 1968 and 1978."

"Yes."

"Strictly speaking, a homicide, is the killing of one person by another. It's a general term applying to noncriminal acts as well as the criminal act, which, of course, is murder."

"Yes. I see."

"Some homicides are considered justifiable, such as the killing of a person to prevent the committing of a serious crime or to assist the police. Or when a person kills in self-defence.'

"I understand."

"So, I take it you don't want information about all homicides in that period—there are dozens—but only those which are either unexplained or we suspect of having been the result of foul play. Am I right?"

"Yes, you are."

"Is there any particular place you want me to start?"

"Yes. The case of a Rosie MacLean, South West Margaree, in June, 1975."

"Let's see...MacLean. R. Yes. Got it. Rose MacLean, aged 13. Death by drowning. Signs of repeatedly being submerged. Pathologists said they couldn't determine how many times, but it would not have been possible for it to have been self-administered. Body discovered under bushes near Collin's Brook. Time of death estimated late afternoon."

"Any clues or suspects?"

"None. Some rumours local lads were involved, but that was pure speculation."

"How far is it from Collin's Brook to Grand Etang?

"Let me see. That's about 33 kilometres. Less than half an hour by car. Why?"

"John Bland was in Grand Etang on that date, and painted a landscape of the scene not far from where he was camping. He could have set his paints to one side, hopped down to Collin's Brook, murdered poor Rosie MacLean and been back at his easel, all in, say, ninety minutes."

"Yes, he could. But *why*, Marc?"

"Because he was a fucking Nazi who specialized in experiments with slow and painful deaths on inmates at Ravensbruck camp!"

"Oh! It's a theory, at least," Patrick said. "And the only one we've got. Give me another case. Let's test that."

"Do you have anything within half an hour's drive of Five Islands Provincial Park on June 10 1969?"

"Yes, by Christ, I do!"

"What is it?"

"Simon Wardle, aged 11. June 10, 1969. Presumed death by injection of substances unknown. The body was unnaturally contorted. It was found in long grass at Riverside Beach near Parrsboro. At first no cause of death was apparent, but examination by the coroner found a needle entry point at base of the skull."

"Clues and suspects?"

"None."

"Bland was camped at Five Islands Park and painted a landscape there. Distance from park to beach?"

"Thirty minutes."

"What do you think?"

"Holy shit! What I think is that we should test a few more and, if they also pan out, I turn it over to my boss for a full-scale investigation."

"Sounds right to me. Okay, try this one. July 31, 1969. Somewhere in the vicinity of Burntcoat Head Park, Noel Shore."

"Hold on a minute. Let me see. Here we go. Oh, Christ! Jacqueline Porter, aged 14. Walton, Hants County. July 21, 1969. Death by repeated application of sulphuric acid. Extensive injuries to 30% of the body, including legs, arms, chest and face. Body discovered by the bank of the Walton River. And before you ask, there were no clues or suspects."

"And how far from there to the Park?"

"Twenty minutes, max."

"Want to try another?"

"I'm already sold. But we may as well. Go ahead."

"Fort Lawrence, July 12, 1977."

"No."

"What do you mean, no?"

"Wait, now. Sorry. Yes. Here's one for July 12, 1977."

"Where?"

"Somewhere called Halfway River."

"Where's that?"

"I'll look it up. Right, here it is. It is about 30 miles south of Amherst."

"That would be, say, 35 minutes from Fort Lawrence. What are the details?"

"Oh my God! You're going to hate this one. Francine McAskill, aged 16. Body discovered near the shore of Newville Lake. Severe injuries to head and all limbs apparently administered by a baseball bat or similar instrument. The weapon was not found. The pathologist determined that the earlier injuries were less severe than subsequent injuries. No suspects."

"Jesus! Any clues?"

"Just one. Remnants of a dye on the victim's clothing. Cadmium red."

"It's him! The bastard!"

"Well, Marc. I think we have a major discovery here. If we can link each of your paintings to a death it will be a fantastic breakthrough which could clear up much of our unsolved list at a stroke."

"I'll say!"

"Now, if you can wait a while, I will have to bring in my Chief Superintendent. He'll have to be briefed and will have to authorize any further action."

"Actually, it is getting a little late for me," I said, "I should be heading for home. Why don't you bring your Chief Super up to date, and why don't Leslie and I come back in a couple of days with all the documents?"

"Who's Leslie?"

"Our researcher. He speaks German, and the documents are written in German."

"What are the documents?"

"There are diaries and notebooks which Bland left behind. These may shed light on his movements and maybe provide details on his victims."

"That'd be great."

"Yes, he should be able to correlate the information from your lists, not only with the paintings and with Bland's diaries, but with his coded notes."

"Okay. Let's meet here in two days at…would ten o'clock be too early?"

"Not for me, but I suspect it would be for Leslie. Can we make it eleven?"

"Let me check with the Chief Super to see if he is available."

While Patrick scurried off along the corridor to the C.S.'s office, I gazed out of the window, observing the shadows gradually lengthen as the day wore on. I thought of the shadows in Bland's painting, which he had later changed, and wondered at the significance of the changes.

Patrick came back, rubbing his hands. "I've never seen the Chief so excited. He says he'll be here at eleven the day after tomorrow, and will be accompanied by a number of other officers. Don't expect me to be in charge, Marc. It's way above my pay grade."

"I hope not," I said. "And by the way, Patrick, I'm being hassled by a Sheridan McCall from the Department of Justice. Do you know him?"

Jeremy Akerman

"Can't say I do. What's it all about?"
"Says I've got to get a private investigator's license."
"Maybe you should."
"You mean turn pro, so to speak?"
"Why not? You never know what adventures lie ahead. Let me make some inquiries. If I can, I'll see what I can find out by the time you come back."

27

The next day, before breakfast, I called Leslie to bring him up to date on my meeting with Patrick Kennedy. I explained how the dates of four of the paintings coincided with murders which had taken place on the same days, not far from the places depicted on the canvases. I also dictated word for word the descriptions of the murders given to me by Kennedy.

"Can you take those descriptions, together with the dates, and see if they will help you crack the code of the notes?" I asked.

"If I take them together with the diaries—which we got from the strong box, and which are not in code—I should be able to."

"If you take the first of the case descriptions and match it with the first of what Bland called 'patient notes', it should give you a head start."

"No, I won't do that, not at first," said Leslie, "I try them at random first, so I won't have my mind prejudiced. Then I will take them in the order of his case notes."

"Excellent. How long do you think it will take you?"

"Depends on the first hour. If it clicks in that time, I could be done by lunch. Don't forget, I've only got four cases out of nine confirmed. If I can't get a handle on it within an hour or two, it could take days."

"Will you call me when—if—you have cracked it, and come to dinner tonight to give us the details?"

"Sure. Sounds good. I've been living on dogs and burgers for the last while."

"I made burgers only the other day."

"You? Chef Snooty? I bet they weren't the usual kind."

"No, you're right. But we won't have them tonight. I have a brace of ducks. Do you like duck?"

"Never had it."

"Never had goose, never had duck! Where have you been all this time?"

"Living the simple life," Leslie said with a laugh. "Look, I'd better get started on this lot. I'll call you the minute I've cracked the code."

For breakfast I made Mimosas with champagne and freshly squeezed orange juice, and eggs Florentine made with spinach Rosalie had picked up at the farmer's market yesterday.

When we had finished eating, I poured us another cup of Kona, a rather special coffee grown in Hawaii which, because of last year's wildfires, had rocketed in price to over $350 per pound.

"So, Bland spelled out the dates on these canvasses—and only on these canvasses—to give himself an alibi for the murders?" Rosalie asked.

"It looks like that. I can't think of any other reason why he would sign these paintings differently from all the others."

"And what about the unfinished—or hurried look—which you noticed from the first time we saw one?"

"Presumably he would allow himself so much time to get from his painting place to the murder sites, but if he miscalculated or if his 'experiments' went wrong somehow, he would be late getting back."

"And would have to rush the endings, ostensibly to finish them before he lost the light."

"Yes, and in the case of *Gathering Storm near Fort Lawrence*, when he got back, he realized that the shadows of the trees were wrong for the time of day he needed for his alibi."

"So he painted over the old shadows and put in new shadows?"

"Yes. It would seem so."

"Even considering the lengths he went to, how did he think he could possibly get away with it for so long?"

"He was a cunning bastard—no mistake about that—and if he had been approached he would probably have said he was some thirty kilometres away from the crime scene and that his painting proved that fact. But, Rosalie, how likely is it that the police would be interested in a highly respected doctor on a camping/painting holiday?"

"Hmm. You know, there is a part of all this I don't understand."

"What part?"

"His camping on his own. Where were his kids all this time?"

"In 1969, the first of our paintings and murders, the girls were already dead, as we know, and Oscar and Edgar were 22 and 21 respectively. It doesn't seem likely they would want to go camping with Daddy, especially not with a freak like Bland."

"I guess not. I wonder what they were doing, and where they were, or if they ever saw or suspected anything."

"We will never know," I said. "Both are long dead."

I made some fresh Kona and took the pot out onto the deck, where Rosalie joined me. My field was looking lush, and at the top of the hill the rows of vines were taking on a coppery tinge. Some bumble bees lazily droned about the buckets of petunias along the edge of the planking, and a curious little finch was hopping about, looking for seeds.

"Have you decided on what you're going to wear to Rachel and Ray's wedding?" I inquired.

"I won't buy anything special," said Rosalie. "If it were a church or synagogue wedding, I might, but I think I'll just wear my pale blue summer dress."

"Good choice. I have that lightweight tan suit," I said, noticing Rosalie had wrinkled her nose up.

"Do you have to?"

"If it's very hot, yes I do."

"Ugh. Makes you look like the Mafia. What if it is cold and cloudy?"

"Then I'll wear a dark suit. Satisfied?"

"I guess so. Marc, who do you think these 'special guests' will be?"

"No clue. There won't be many family on either side. Maybe someone from his political side."

"Ray? Political?"

"Yes, he was a big wheel in one of the parties for years. The special guests will probably be the local MLA and his wife."

I poured us some more coffee, then strolled inside and took the ducks out of the freezer. In this heat and humidity it would not take long for them to thaw. I thought I would slow roast them, something I know many chefs would deplore because they had all climbed on the pink meat band wagon. I have nothing against pink beef or lamb, but I think pink duck really tastes more like beef than duck. Duck needs the cooking time for the delicious fat to envelop and penetrate the flesh.

With the duck I would gently sauté some leaks with mushrooms to serve with tiny potatoes. For a sauce, I thought that a delicate blend of pureed plums, ginger and soy would do.

In the cellar I had half a case of 2005 Musigny from Domaine Jacques-Frederic Mugnier, so I headed down to and extracted a bottle. I intended to serve smoked salmon to start, and to accompany that I selected a bottle of 2010 Corton Charlemagne from Louis Latour.

As I was coming up for the cellar, I heard the phone ringing.

"Marc, it's for you. It's Leslie."

"Leslie. Any luck?"

"It really is a very simple code once you have a few salient features. It worked out faster than I expected. I can now match the notes, the diary entries, and the paintings with the murders,"

"Great! Come to dinner and explain it to us."

"Marc, I'm not sure. I mean, I've love to come and eat your duck, but...."

"But what?"

"The notes, once decoded—"

"Yes?"

"They're not the sort of thing you want to read at the dinner table."

"That bad?"

"Fucking horrendous. If this guy wasn't already dead, I'd kill him myself with my bare hands."

"Let me consult with Rosalie. I call you right back."

I explained the situation to Rosalie.

Initially, her face fell, but, having thought for a second or two, she finally spoke. "Thing is," she said, "We're signed up to this. We can't just walk away."

"I know. That's a given. The question is, do we want to hear this depraved stuff before or after eating, or at some other time?"

"When do we have to have to see Kennedy and his boss?"

"Tomorrow at eleven."

"Then we have no choice. But let's do it after dinner."

"OK. I'll call Leslie back. Then I'll call Ray."

Ray and Rachel picked up Leslie in town and arrived a little after six thirty. We socialized for a while, drinking champagne, then, in a fairly subdued mood, sat down and enjoyed dinner.

The duck was particularly juicy and tasty and went extremely well with the Musigny. Nobody felt like dessert, and we all wanted to get on with the unpleasant business of the moment.

"Right," I said, after we had moved into the living room. "We have only four cases to consider tonight, and when we meet with Kennedy tomorrow there will be another five cases on the agenda."

"Before we start, I have a question," Rachel said.

"Yes, Rachel?"

"If Bland was apparently killing people on a regular basis between 1969 and 1978, why don't we have any cases in 1971 or 1972?"

"I think I have the answer to that," said Leslie. "Those summers were particularly wet. It rained for weeks on end. I am guessing, with the demands of his practice, he just had to cancel his camping plans."

"How about 1974?" Rosalie said. "I don't think we have a murder that year. Why not?"

"Ah, yes, the answer is in the diaries, too. He sprained his ankle and had to stay close to home. Camping and running around murdering people would not have been possible."

"And I guess we have no idea how his victims were selected," Ray said. "We don't know if they happened to be in those locations by chance, as it were, or if he had somehow scouted their whereabouts ahead of time?"

"No. There's nothing in the diaries or the notes to suggest either *modus operandi*," said Leslie. "For all we know, it might have been a mixture of methods."

"My guess would be that they were random," said Rachel. "He wouldn't have had the time to go scouting. He probably decided what 'experiment' he would conduct on a particular camping trip, but had to take what victims became available."

"Leslie," I said, trying to bring matters to a head, "the first case we have information for is 1969. The painting is called *Five Islands Provincial Park*. The murder of Simon Wardle was on the same date at Riverside Beach near Parrsboro, only thirty minutes' drive away. The police report said the body was unusually contorted and death was by injection of unknown substances. What can you tell us?"

"You're not going to like this." He read from his notes:

Fall Eins. Giftspritze. Unterschiedliche Mengen an Pancuroniumbromid und Kaliumchlorid. Tod in 24 Minuten.
Case One. Lethal Injection. Varying levels of pancuroniam bromide and potassium chloride. Death in 24 minutes.
Caught the victim unawares and gave him a small injection to immobilize him. Then I injected a number of very small doses of the potassium chloride directly into the spinal column. This produced severe, extremely painful cramps in the lower limbs, pruritus, and sweating, paraplegia and likely hyperkalemia. The levels of pain varied, as expected, but at times approximated near death tolerance when time was allowed prior to next injection. The patient took longer to die than anticipated and that it was only after I had made a sufficient number of observations that I dispatched the patient with a larger dose of potassium chloride.

"Thank you Leslie," I said very quickly, to avoid our getting being overtaken by emotion and revulsion. "The next case, also in 1969. The painting is called *Burntcoat Head Park*. The murder of Jaqueline Porter was on the same date, her body being discovered on the banks of the River Walton, some twenty minutes away by car. The police report says death occurred as a result of repeated application of sulphuric acid. Leslie?"

"Yes, Marc. Here goes:"

Fall Zwei. Schwefelsäure. Das junge Mädchen war schlank

und hatte ein schwaches Wesen. Tod in 44 Minuten.

Case Two. Sulphuric acid. Young girl was of slim build and weak disposition. Death in 44 minutes.

I bound her to a tree and applied small doses. Initial application was to the feet, then to limbs, then trunk. Final applications were to face and genitals. A gag consisting of a large handkerchief was necessary due to loudness of the patient's cries. As expected, pain increased with number and type of application, and several times the patient was almost lost before the end of the experiment.

Rosalie cried out and rushed from the room. I could hear her sobbing in the kitchen.

"Do we really have to go on?" Leslie asked, almost begging.

"We have to," Rachel said solemnly. "Don't forget we have to do these again, and another five, tomorrow."

"That's true," said Ray. "We may as well get used to it now."

"Take a quick break," said Rachel. "I'll go and talk to Rosalie."

I poured us all large Cognacs to sustain us. We had two more cases to go through tonight, and I knew none of us would have an easy time of it. I hoped, or perhaps feared, that we would become numbed or case-hardened as we proceeded.

The women came back into the room and sat down. Rosalie took a large slug of Cognac, sniffed, and smiled heroically.

"Sorry gang," she said. "Won't happen again."

"Right, Leslie. The next case is June 1975. The painting was called *Grand Etang, Cabot Trail*. The body of Rose Maclean was discovered in bushes at Collin's Brook, less than 33 kilometres from Grand Etang. The police report said she had been drowned but in a way which could not have been self- administered."

Fall sieben. Ertrinken. Sehr gebrechliches Mädchen etwa 12 Jahre. Tod in 38 Minuten.

Case Seven. Drowning. Very frail girl about 12 years. Death in 38 minutes.

Little difficulty was encountered in overpowering the patient and in subsequently maintaining absolute control. Patient was submerged until life was felt to be in danger, then withdrawn and resuscitated. Repeated applications of this treatment continued, until it became clear the patient was too weak to continue and was allowed to expire. Remarkable levels of pain were observed throughout the experiment.

"Oh God!" said Ray.

"We must move on," I said reluctantly, "Only one more to go."

"I should warn you," Leslie said. "This one is the worst."

"Thanks for warning us. So, this case is July, 1977. The painting was our old friend *Gathering Storm near Fort Lawrence*. The body of 16-year-old Francine MacAskill was found near the shore of Neville Lake, Cumberland County, approximately 35 minutes away. The police report said she had sustained multiple injuries of varying severity administered by a baseball bat or similar instrument. The weapon was not recovered.

Fall Nummer neun. Trauma durch stumpfe Gewalteinwirkung. Mollige junge Frau um die 17. Tod in 47 Minuten.

Case number nine. Blunt force trauma. Chubby young woman around 17. Death in 57 minutes.

Some difficulty was experienced securing patient in position. Then force was administered slowly, lesser blows preceding harder, later blows, in the following order: Toes, feet, fingers, hands, legs, arms, knees, elbows, torso and head.

187

Surprisingly high levels of pain achieved over remarkably lengthy period. This latter was facilitated by amount of subcutaneous fat which was why the patient was chosen.

"Jesus Christ!" Ray exploded.

"*Oy, gott im himmel*," said Rachel quietly.

"Is that it, Leslie?"

"Yes, Marc. Thank God I have no more. Although we will hear more like this—perhaps even worse—tomorrow at the RCMP headquarters."

"Thank you, Leslie," said Ray, still visibly shaking. "It can't have been easy for you."

"No, it wasn't." Leslie said. "I don't mind telling you, Ray, that if I'd known what I was getting into, I would never have agreed to do this. Marc, can I have another drink?"

"Sure, I think we could all use one," I said, circulating with the Cognac decanter. "You can all stay here tonight and we can go up to Dartmouth from here, if that's all right with everybody. We have plenty of rooms, toiletries and even changes of clothes."

"I'll go and get the things you'll need," said Rosalie.

As she got up I noticed she had been crying again.

We finished our drinks and went to our various rooms almost in silence. A few, muted goodnights were exchanged.

28

Getting everybody up in time the next morning and feeding them was quite a task. Fortunately, we have four bathrooms so there were no queues or shouts of "hurry up!" or "What are you doing in there?", and soon we were all seated around the large table where we had dinner the previous evening.

I cut and toasted two loaves of sourdough bread and whipped up 20 fresh eggs with thick cream and chopped chives. While I made scrambled eggs in a big skillet, Rosalie got two pots of coffee going.

"Ray, if it's okay with you," I said, "I think we should all travel together in your car."

"Sure. We have lots of room."

"When we get there, how will we proceed?" Rachel asked.

"I'm not exactly sure. The Chief Super said there would be a number of officers present."

"They won't try and exclude Ray and me, will they?"

"Good God, I should think not!" Rosalie said. "Leastways, they better not try!"

"I hadn't thought of that," I said, "They could hardly exclude Ray or Leslie, but I guess they might try to keep the rest of us out."

"That would be outrageous!"

Just then the telephone rang and I went into the kitchen to answer it.

"LeBlanc."

"Mark, it's Patrick."

"Good morning, Patrick. What's going on?"

"I'm calling from home. I wanted to give you a heads-up about a few things before you come here today."

"Oh yes?"

"First, I checked up on your friend Sheridan McCall."

"And what did you find?"

"He's not with the provincial Department of Justice, as he led you to believe. He's a fed."

"A fed! Then why was he pushing me to get a private investigator's license?"

"I guess that was part of the subterfuge. Or to scare you. He works for the Minister of Public Safety."

"Isn't that the minister the RCMP reports to?"

"Yes. Our Commissioner reports directly to the minister."

"Any idea what he was looking for?"

"I don't, but something else has come up. I can't say if there is any connection."

"What?"

"The information you gave me on anti-Semites at Acadia—especially on Mr. Shaw?"

"What about it?"

"My Super told me last night I am not to pursue investigations on that subject."

"Really? Do you know why?"

"No, he didn't say. I am a lowly inspector. I can't question his decisions."

"I don't like the sound of this. Anything else?"

"Yes. I won't be in the meeting today."

"Why not?"

"It's been taken out of our hands. My Chief Super will be present, but he'll be the only one from H-Division."

"Damn! Then who will be there?"

"S Division."

"What the hell is that?"

"Officially, it doesn't exist. I presume it took over from the old S and I Division when CSIS was formed."

"What does it do?"

"I don't know, and even if I did I couldn't tell you. All I know is that CSIS can investigate but does not have to power to arrest or detain and does not enforce the Criminal Code or other laws."

"So you're telling me these guys are the Heavy Mob?"

"No, I'm telling you nothing."

"Anything else to make my day? Will they try to exclude Rachel, Rosalie or me from the meeting?"

"They might, but I don't know. But when you arrive, they're going to split you up."

"What?"

"At least for the first hour, they want Mr. Alsop by himself."

"Leslie! Why? Are we being treated as criminals?"

"No, not at all. They just want their man to sit down with Alsop and go through the code business."

"Who is this guy?"

"I don't know him, but apparently his name is Henrich Braun."

"A German?"

"I don't know. But they need to be satisfied that their translator has more or less the same take on these cases."

"If that's the case, we needn't be there at eleven. We could drop off Leslie and come back later."

"Marc. Please don't do that. I beg you not to do anything foolish."

"Now you're starting to scare me."

"You should be scared. These guys have sweeping powers and they don't fool around. I don't know what their angle is, and I don't want to know. You and I will never discuss this again. Understood?"

"Jesus!"

"In fact, Marc, we have never discussed it. Right?"

"Right."

I waited a full five minutes after hanging up on Patrick, debating whether I should tell the others. If I did tell them, their actions on arrival might betray the fact that they had prior knowledge of the RCMP's intentions and it might cause serious trouble for Patrick.

I decided to confine my disclosure to the information about Sheridan McCall and leave it at that.

We got on the road in good time, and had a leisurely drive to Dartmouth. Rosalie, Leslie and I were scrunched into the back seat (I loathe travelling in the back seat) and were in a sombre mood.

Rachel cleared her throat. "I hope you won't mind my saying something about last night?"

"No, why should we mind?" Rosalie asked.

"It's just that I wondered if you thought I wasn't affected by what we learned."

"No," Leslie said. "Although I did think you took it a lot better than the rest of us."

"Why do you suppose that was, Leslie? What we were told last night were the acts of a vicious, calculating, heartless man, but they were not the acts of a madman."

"How do you mean?"

"To call him a madman would be to excuse his misdeeds. To you, he is a hideous but rare character who has made his way into your lives. But to my people, his kind is all too common. There are many thousands like him. Jews have been enduring his kind since time immemorial. So, if we seem to deal with these revelations with a brave face, it doesn't mean we don't feel it even more keenly than you do."

~

We arrived at H-Division headquarters, parked the car and registered at the desk. Our information was relayed by the receptionist to someone within the building and soon an officer, a very severe-looking Sergeant Major, appeared and asked us to follow him.

On the second floor, he led us into a large conference room and asked us to be seated at the end of the table.

"Not you, Mr. Alsop. You must come with me."

"What?"

"Why?"

"Where are you taking him?"

"I have orders to escort Mr. Alsop to our translation wing. You will be reunited with him in about an hour."

Leslie got up reluctantly, grabbed his backpack and shuffled towards the door. "I guess I'll see you guys later," he said sheepishly.

The Sergeant Major ushered Leslie out of the door and then leaning back to us, winked. "Be careful what you say. The room is bugged," he said with a grin.

"The damned thing," Ray said when the Sergeant Major had gone, "is that he's probably telling the truth. I'll bet the place *is* bugged. So we'd better take care we don't make any silly remarks we might later regret."

It was one of the longest hours I had ever endured. We had no reading material and none of us felt like indulging in small talk, especially not after Ray's admonitions.

Eventually, we heard some noise out in the corridor and the door opened to admit five men, two women, and Leslie who, looking quite pleased with himself, wandered down to our end of the table.

The only one in uniform was the Chief Superintendent of H-Division, whom I recognized by the crown and two diamonds on his epaulettes. Of the others, the only one I had seen before was Sheridan McCall—if that was his real name.

One of the men, a stout sixty-year-old wearing a herringbone suit, took the centre chair at the opposite end of the table from us. He was flanked by a stern, middle-aged woman who looked like a librarian and a thin, severe man in his thirties who wore rimless glasses. Next to the first woman was a much older lady, rather like someone's grandmother, and, on the other side sat McCall, looking like the cat that got the cream. The other two men sat at some distance from their colleagues, almost as if they were representing another party at the session.

"There is no need for introductions since we know who you all are," said the man in the herringbone suit. "The only person we will need to identify is Mr. Henrich Braun, whom we shall be calling upon frequently."

One of the men at the side of the table stiffly inclined his head.

"We wish to acknowledge the excellent work which has been conducted by Mr. Leslie Alsop, to which we will also be making continual reference."

Leslie bowed his head and was positively preening.

"With minor amendments, Mr. Braun has confirmed Mr. Alsop's translation of the relevant patient notes, so we need not go over them again. We accept as an overwhelming probability that Francine McAskill, Jacqueline Porter, Rose MacLean and Simon Wardle were murdered by Walter Eugen Klemper, alias John Bland."

McCall stretched out with his feet sticking out under the table. The grandmother polished her glasses with a Kleenex. The librarian and the severe thin man stared ahead, motionless and without expression.

"Mr. Braun, can you give us the patient notes attached to June 13, 1970? The case of Stephen King, aged nine. Body discovered at Greenfield, Hants County. The painting is *Rawdon Gold Mines*."

"Thank you, Mr. Chairman." Braun spoke with a slight but noticeable German accent. "Case Number Three. Young boy. Death in 18 minutes. Patient was easy to overcome and bind. Electric shocks were administered via car battery. Experiment was unsuccessful because the degree of electrical current could not be regulated. Will need to repeat."

"That agrees with the police report," the Chairman said. "To save my asking each time, if any of you has any doubt as to the authorship of these murders, please speak up following each of Mr. Braun's presentations.

"July 25, 1970. Angela Waybrett aged 12. Body discovered at Eel Bay. The painting is *Clyde River Campsite*."

"Mr. Chairman. Case Number Four. Young woman in good health. Death in 24 minutes. Purpose of experiment was to assess effects on humans of chlorine trifluoride. Substance was difficult to administer due to its extreme volatility. After three trials the patient's clothing caught fire and ill-considered attempts to extinguish with water produced a violent reaction resulting in severe chemical and thermal burns. Experiment was unsuccessful but will not be repeated."

"Again not inconsistent with the police report," intoned herringbone. "June 24, 1972. Wayne Googoo, aged 4. Body discovered near Eskasoni. The painting is *Ben Eoin*."

"Case Number Five. Young boy. Undernourished appearance. Hemotoxin. Death in 23 minutes. Purpose of experiment was to succeed where Dr Karl Schmidt had failed in 1957. The toxin, product of the boomslang snake, was exceedingly difficult to obtain. After initial application the patient became confused and nauseated, exhibiting signs of small clots forming in the blood until the ability to clot further was lost. Patient expired as a result of internal and external bleeding."

"Right. Moving on. August 2, 1973. Regina Macleod, aged 12.

Body discovered at New Harris. The painting is *Seal Island Bridge*."

"Case Number Six," Mr. Braun announced. "Teenage girl. Very strong for her age. Strangulation. Death in 28 minutes. Patient was uncooperative and struggled continuously. It was apparent, however, that considerable levels of pain were experienced prior to the patient expiring."

"Consistent with police reports," said herringbone. "And finally, Mr. Braun, we have August 13, 1976. John Rathbone aged 17. Body found near Deep Brook. The painting is *Bear River*."

"Yes, sir. Case Number Eight. Young man, fit and in good health but simple in mind. Death in 34 minutes. Sought to engage in fisticuffs as a game, but patient proved stronger and more adept than had been foreseen. Was forced to dispatch patient by means of automobile tire iron."

"Thank you, Mr. Braun. You may go," said herringbone, perfunctorily.

Once Braun was out the door, he continued, "The reports on cases One, Two, Seven and Nine which are Mr. Alsop's translations corroborated by Mr. Braun, you have in front of you. There is one question for us to determine immediately. Were all these previously unsolved murders the work of one man?"

There were murmurs of assent around the table.

"And were they the work of Werner Eugen Klemper, alias John Bland?"

Again there was nodding and sounds of agreement.

"Very well. Accordingly, I instruct Chief Superintendent Clarkson to declare these unsolved cases officially solved and to relegate the files appropriately. We thank you for your time and attention, Chief Superintendent. You may now leave us."

As the Chief Superintendent was leaving, the man who had been sitting at the side of the table moved around to our group and placed a piece of paper in front of each of us. As he did so, the grandmother followed him and gently, but forcibly, relieved Leslie of the contents of his backpack.

"What the hell is this?" demanded Ray.

"Yeah. Why is she taking my stuff?" Leslie whined.

"Ladies and gentlemen," said herringbone, "the proceedings of this meeting and all documents pertaining to it are now deemed to be subject to the Security of Information Act 1985 C-05, otherwise known as the Official Secrets Act. The Minister of Public Safety," he inclined his head towards Sheridan McCall, nodded with a smile, "has adjudged this to be a matter of National Security."

"What the fuck!" Ray was now standing.

"You are all required to say nothing of this meeting to any other person, nor anything of what you have learned during your investigations of this matter, on pain of indictment with penalties up to 14 years' imprisonment. Now, please sign the paper in front of you, indicating your agreement to abide by the rules of the Act."

"And if we don't?" Rosalie demanded.

"Then you will be detained and prosecuted forthwith *in camera*."

"But why?" I asked.

"I'm very sorry, but I am not permitted to tell you any more than I already have. Believe me, I understand your predicament, but my hands are tied."

"You won't even tell us who you are?"

"Alas, no. Please sign. It is for the best."

We sat in silence for a few seconds, looking at each other.

Finally, Rachel spoke, very softly but sadly. "You knew it would come to this. After the crimes, always the cover ups. Sign, sign. We have no choice."

~

The sun was blazing own when we came out. It was now afternoon. Everything around us seemed normal. I felt as if I had just escaped from a Kafka novel.

As we climbed into Ray's BMW, a nasty thought occurred to me. "Don't be surprised if we find our places have been raided when we get home."

"They wouldn't, would they?" Rosalie said.

"You heard Old Herringbone. All records pertaining to the case are the property of the government."

"They'll have a job getting into our house," she said, "with that security system."

"There's nothing at our house," I said. "All materials were at Ray's or with Leslie."

"Shit!" Ray cursed. "All the work everybody's done for me, and I don't even have a private record of my own grandfather's devilish escapades."

Leslie spluttered.

"What?"

"I made copies of the diaries," he said with a smirk. "I'll let you have them when the smoke has settled."

"Good man!" I said, "But won't they find them?"

"Not unless they want to go riffling through my mother's panty drawer."

"Well done, Leslie!" Rachel cried. "Are there many of them we haven't seen?"

"Oh, sure. We pretty much only looked at the early pages, and then those dealing with the dates of the paintings. There's loads of stuff even I haven't looked at."

"Let's allow things to settle for a week," I said. "Then you go and get them from your Mum's panty drawer, have a look through and, if there's anything interesting, let us know and we'll gather for dinner."

"Sounds good to me. I like eating your dinners."

"I thought they were too 'snooty' for you."

"I am getting to be a little snooty myself," Leslie said with a laugh.

"Why don't you bring your pal Henrich Braun with you?"

"That creep! Where'd they find him, I wonder."

"Yes, I wondered that too," Rachel said very quietly.

Jeremy Akerman

29

I awoke in the middle of the night, struck by the realization that I had inadvertently spoken a mistruth in the car on the way home from Dartmouth. I had completely forgotten that I still had the Bland diaries in my biometric safe and had made copies which I had then given to Leslie.

I had to get out of bed and go downstairs and check in the safe to make sure of this. When I did so, I found the diaries were indeed there.

Leslie told us he had made copies and hidden them in his mother's panty drawer. If that were true, he must have made copies of the copies. My wondering why he would do that, and not tell us, kept me awake for at least another hour, and when I finally drifted off I was still none the wiser. But it did mean, of course, that I could expect a visit from the RCMP soon to take the diaries into custody.

Sure enough, even before breakfast the next morning, they were knocking on our door and demanding documents.

I willingly gave them everything I had, but exploded when they said they would need to take Rosalie's laptop as well. Understandably, she was also upset, and we only calmed down slightly when the staff sergeant said he did not have to take it away if we would give him somewhere to sit and check it out.

While two other officers were rummaging around the house, he went to work and, after an hour, announced that anything pertinent had been removed. They thanked us politely and, bearing the diaries, now sealed in a special case, left us alone.

I called Ray to warn him, but they had already been to his house and taken everything he had in a number of boxes. They also took the paintings, for which they gave him a receipt, saying they would be returned to him 'in due course.'

Then I called Leslie, who had only just got up.

"Have the Heavy Mob been yet? They've been to Ray's earlier and just left here."

"No, I haven't seen anyone. They might be on their way here."

"Well, you are warned." I hesitated. "Leslie…?"

"Yeah?"

"You never had the original diaries. I kept them in my safe and gave you copies."

"Yeah."

"In the car you said you made a copy and hid one of them in your mother's panty drawer."

"No, I didn't."

"Yes, you did."

"Did I? I must have been confused. You know, after being shut up with Henrich Braun and all, I guess my head wasn't on straight."

"So, are you saying you have only one copy of the diaries?"

"Yes. No. That is, only one I'll give to the cops to keep them happy. It's too early, Marc, I haven't woken up yet."

"So, there are two copies?"

"Yeah, I guess so."

"And the one you won't give to the cops is the one you are going to check out and report back to us by the weekend?"

"Sure."

"Okay. Expect a visit from the law any minute."

I came away from the conversation even more puzzled and perturbed than I was before. Was Leslie really confused by events and by not being fully awake?

Rosalie and I had still not had breakfast and were in foul moods. I cooked a few eggs and we just had them with coffee.

When I told her about Leslie, she could not make any sense of it either.

"How did you get hold of Leslie in the first place?" I asked.

"I don't remember. I think he was recommended by someone at the university."

"You don't remember who?"

"No, I don't. I remember being told he was a graduate student with outstanding marks and fully fluent in German."

"Did you go to the German Department to find him?"

"It would be the Languages and Literature Department, but no, I didn't. Whoever gave me the tip told where he lived and I tracked him down there."

"Do me a favour, darling. Call the department and ask if they expect him in today."

"Okay. I'll be right back."

I think I knew what was coming. When things don't add up, there is seldom a simple explanation. Where the strange behaviour of people is concerned, I had learned that the answer is usually unpleasant.

"You'll never guess," Rosalie said as she came back.

"They've never heard of Leslie Alsop?"

"Yes, how did you know?"

"I guessed. No sign of him at all?"

"No."

"I know it won't do any good, but I'll call him right now."

As I anticipated, in the space of less than an hour, his telephone had been disconnected.

I called Ray and put him in the picture.

"Son of a bitch!" he said. "He sure won't be getting the other half of his pay!"

"Somehow, Ray, I rather think that not getting his money is the least of his concerns."

"What the hell do you think he was playing at, Marc?"

"I have no clue. I am guessing that when he went off into that room with Braun, they had coffee with their colleagues."

"You think he's a fed?"

"Make sense, but I really don't know."

"Jesus."

"Ray…"

"Yes?"

"You should put all this stuff behind you and concentrate on having a marvellous wedding."

"You're right. I'm sure Rachel will agree."

"We'll still be seeing each other. Why don't we get together on the weekend?"

"That sounds nice. No mystery, no drama, no frigging Nazis. Just friends and dinner."

"You've got it. Rosalie and I will look forward to it."

Later in the day I swung by Leslie's boarding house. I knew I wouldn't find him there, but I had to do it.

The Chinese student who answered the door did not know who Leslie was, and when I described him he shook his head. I asked him if he knew or had heard of the infamous Shaw, but I drew another blank.

So I drove back into town and went to see Louise at the wine store. I was amazed and very pleased with what she had accomplished with the place; it looked gorgeous and the products were displayed to their best advantage, being lighted beautifully. I was even more pleased to learn that she had now acquired enough stock to sell to the public, and was planning a Grand Opening event within the next two days.

I told her what a wonderful job she had done and gave her the date of Rachel and Ray's wedding, asking her to get a case of very special Champagne, Laurent-Perrier Alexandra Grande Cuvée Rosé 2004, which I considered to be a lovely expression of elegance and love. I thought it would be the perfect wedding present for two fine people.

I then crossed the street and went into the book shop to see Gerald, who began fussing all over me. He told me the business was fine and that he was experiencing no particular problems. He had, he said, moved out of his flat and was now living in my father's old apartment above the shop.

He asked me if I still wanted him to keep an eye out for any books about wartime Nazis in the Annapolis Valley, and I told him not to bother. He said he had come across one book—more of a leaflet really—by an official who had been in Canadian Counter-Intelligence during the war.

"It's quite interesting, Marc. He says a German spy landed here in the 1940s."

"Really? May I have it?"

"Certainly. I got it for you."

I quickly thumbed through it. Clearly, the author knew what he was talking about and the publication was filled with footnotes.

I came to a chapter entitled *U-boat and Spies*, and read it with great interest. It described the journey of the *Feinste* and the spy who was brought to Canada aboard her. There was a photograph of him. He was short, dark and unprepossessing. He had been a lieutenant in the Wehrmacht. His name was Helmut Schultz.

As I returned to the Bugatti, my mind was reeling. First the RCMP and the Official Secrets Act, then Leslie, and now this. What on earth did it all mean? I wondered what other surprises could possibly be in store.

30

As planned, when Saturday came around we accepted an invitation to go to Rachel and Ray's house for the evening.

From the minute we set foot inside the door, Rosalie and I could tell something was wrong. You could cut the air with a knife. At first, we were worried that Ray and Rachel had had an argument which did not seem propitious for the coming wedding, but Ray quickly put our suspicions to rest.

"Poor Rachel," he said. "She's very upset by something in today's news. And even more upset that she can't do anything about it."

"What it is, Rachel?" said Rosalie kindly. "You can tell us."

"It's more of the same. A relentless onslaught. I get so angry about it, yet at the same time very weary."

"You may have seen it on television," said Ray. "It's a story about two Haredi children spitting at English tourists."

"What are Haredi?" Rosalie asked.

"They are groups within Orthodox Judaism who observe strict adherence to Halakla (that's Jewish law) and traditions," said Rachel, "They're usually referred to as ultra-Orthodox to convey the impression that they are wild-eyed fanatics. Haredi like to think of themselves as the most religiously authentic Jews."

"Ah, I see. What did these children do?"

"The news says they spat at English 'tourists', as Ray just did, but what they didn't say is that they weren't tourists at all. They were members of an extremist so-called Christian mission to 'spread the truth' to Jews in Israel. They are troublemakers who go to the Haredi neighbourhoods and deliberately provoke the inhabitants, saying that the Talmud is an 'evil book'."

"Why didn't the news tell the whole story?"

"Because they want to make Jews look bad. Let's face it, the kids were wrong. They should not have behaved like that, but wouldn't orthodox religious people anywhere be mad if someone comes to their house or synagogue and insults them?"

"I see your point," I said.

"That video claiming to show Christian women tourists being abused by Orthodox children got over nine million views."

"Without telling the whole story." Ray added.

"Every Jewish school and synagogue has CCTV cameras to protect them against anti-Semites. But for every one of them hundreds of others are used to lure Jews into situations so they can be portrayed in a bad light."

"Not fair," said Rosalie.

"The same day," Rachel continued, "a Christian was burned alive in Nigeria, a Christian family faced death for blasphemy in Pakistan, a dozen Christians were murdered in Burkina Faso, a young Hindu girl was stolen from her home and married off to a 40-year-old Muslim. There was no mention of any of these outrages in the western media."

"Almost every week, it's the same," said Ray. "Sometimes, it's every day."

"Jews are the only people on earth who are expected to be perfect citizens on their best behaviour twenty-four hours a day, and if they are not the cameras will always be rolling. Whether it's CBC, ATV, BBC or Amnesty International, they are on a constant look-out for opportunities to pounce and try to make Jews look bad."

"I didn't know any of this until I met Rachel," said Ray sadly.

"And we're just learning how biased the media is," I said.

"Let's have some bubble and put the cares of the world behind us for a few hours," Ray said. "I have some Dom Perignon chilling."

The company cheered up at this announcement, and even more at the news that Rachel had prepared borscht with sour cream, roast chicken with knishes and red cabbage, and chocolate babkas for dinner.

Ray told us he had a Grich Hills Chardonnay 2012 to start and a Chateau Musar 2005 to go with the main course. This latter was a curiously good wine made from the Obaideh and Merwah grapes in the Beqaa Valley of Lebanon. Despite much fighting and turmoil in the area, the winery had managed to put out quality products since 1930. So turbulent had been the district that some experts claimed they could smell cordite in the wine!

The meal was delicious, the wines very good and the company was marvellous.

Rosalie, who had perhaps drunk a little too much, proposed a toast. "You guys have become our best friends. Here's to best friends!"

"We feel the same way," said Rachel. "I second the toast!"

"I will third it," I said.

"And I will fourth it," Ray cried.

We laughed heartily and drank deeply of the smoky, dark red wine.

Suddenly, the front door bell rang.

"Who can that be at this time of night?" Rachel wondered.

"We'll soon find out," said Ray, getting up from the table.

We heard his footsteps to the door, and the door open, but no voices. Then we heard gravel scrunching as Ray walked out into the forecourt.

The door slammed shut and he walked slowly into the room, holding a manila envelope.

"Who was it, Ray?" Rachel asked.

"Nobody. I went out to look around, but couldn't see anyone. Then as I came back in I saw this lying on the doormat."

"What is it?"

"Don't know. Let's open it and see."

He slit down the envelope with his table knife, then extracted something written on pale blue paper. "Son of a bitch!"

"What?"

"It's from Leslie."

"Leslie?!"

"'You won't need me to say who this is from, so I won't,'" read Ray.

> I reckon you must be mad at me, and I want to say I am sorry about the way we had to part company. I won't go into how and why they got to me, or why I had no choice but to collaborate, because it would serve no useful purpose.
>
> But when Marc talked to me that morning I knew my cover was blown and I had to clear out fast. I wouldn't have tried to get in touch now except for two reasons.
>
> The first is I want to say I hope you and Rachel have a wonderful wedding, and that you have all the happiness in the world in your marriage.
>
> The second—and this is **most important**—is that I have discovered something which it is vital that you, Ray, be aware of.
>
> You may remember my saying we had only studied those parts of Bland's diaries which concerned the early years and the years of the murders. Since we returned from Dartmouth, I have had a chance to read the other pages. Most of them make boring reading at best, and unpleasant reading at worst. There are a few entries, however, which I felt you had a right to know about. This is the operative passage:

January 2nd 1988. I called on Edgar, and found him and Grace squabbling in a highly unseemly fashion. I had to strike both of them across their faces to get them to stop shouting. When I demanded to know the reason for the commotion, I managed to extract an utterly disgraceful explanation. Grace is pregnant, a farmer from Billtown being the father rather than my son. I am furious with her and struck her again to show my displeasure. I refuse to countenance any discussion of abortion or separation, or any public acknowledgement of the facts. I ordered them to make the best of the situation and continue as if nothing has happened. The child is to be reared as Edgar's and will be told nothing of Grace's misbehaviour. My useless son and his wretched wife are a continuing burden to me, especially when I have important work to attend to.

So, you see, Ray, John Bland—or whatever his name was—was **not** your grandfather. Your grandfather was some unknown peasant!

I hope this comes as agreeable news. I imagine Rachel will find it particularly satisfying.

Best wishes to you both. Also to Rosalie and Marc. We shall not meet again.

"Good heavens above!" cried Rosalie in astonishment.
"See, Rachel," said Ray, "I'm not a Nazi after all. Aren't you glad?"
"Very glad, my darling," she said, embracing him fondly.

Jeremy Akerman

31

The wedding was everything everybody had hoped for. The day was sunny and bright, but not too hot, the bride was beautiful, the groom was handsome, the service was dignified yet humorous, the party was humming, the drink was first class and the food was outstanding.

There were only about twenty at the Town Hall for the service, neither Rachel nor Ray having any relatives within travelling distance, so just close friends and special guests were present. Rabbi Karlin and Chedva Bensai came, together with the Premier of Nova Scotia, Wendell Proctor, and his wife Cynthia.

The premier stood out because of his extreme height and his handsome blackness, and his wife by her genteel beauty and winning smile.

After the ceremony, conducted remarkably well by Walter Bryden, we all went to Port Williams, where an immense marquee had been erected on the Blands' lawn.

To this part of the wedding event, it seemed, half the town and most of the county had been invited. A table veritably glittering with gifts stood near the flower beds, the LeBlancs' case of special rosé Champagne prominent among them.

For their honeymoon, the Blands would be going to Israel to see Rachel's relatives. Then they would fly to Palermo in Sicily, rent a car, and drive up through Italy to Venice, *La Serenisima*. From there they intended to fly to Paris and have a week there before returning home. It was obvious to all that this was a couple who were made for each other and, further, that they would turn out to be pillars of the community for years to come.

Just before they left for the airport, the couple wandered through the crowd, thanking people for their attendance. When they got to where Rosalie and I were standing, Ray grinned and gave the thumbs up.

Rachel hugged Rosalie and kissed me on the cheek. "*Ale gut vos ends gezunt,*" she said.

"*Loybn Got,*" I said.

"You're learning." She laughed.

"There are still a lot of unanswered questions," I said. "Does that bother you?"

"We may find out some day. We may not," said Rachel. "*Es iz got's vet.*"

"I can live with it," said Ray, "but there is one thing that really bugs me."

"What's that, Ray?"

"If John Bland wasn't who we thought he was, then who the hell *was* he?"

Jeremy Akerman

Acknowledgements

Yet again I record my grateful thanks to my wife, Caroll Anne, for her support and encouragement throughout the writing of this book. She read each chapter as it was written and made many useful suggestions for improvement.

Jeremy Akerman

About the author

Jeremy Akerman is an adoptive Nova Scotian who has lived in the province since 1964. In that time he has been an archaeologist, a radio announcer, a politician, a senior civil servant, a newspaper editor and a film actor.
    He is painter of landscapes and portraits, a singer of Irish folk songs, a lover of wine, and a devotee of history, especially of the British Labour Party.